Here's what teens are saying about Bluford High:

"I love the Bluford series because I can relate to the stories and the characters. They are just like real life. Ever since I read the first one, I've been hooked."
—*Jolene P.*

"All the Bluford books are great. There wasn't one that I didn't like, and I read them all—twice!"
—*Sequoyah D.*

"I found it very easy to lose myself in these books. They kept my interest from beginning to end and were always realistic. The characters are vivid, and the endings left me in eager anticipation of the next book."
—*Keziah J.*

"As soon as I finished one book, I couldn't wait to start the next one. No books have ever made me do that before."
—*Terrance W.*

"Each Bluford book gives you a story that could happen to anyone. The details make you feel like you are inside the books. The storylines are amazing and realistic. I loved them all."
—*Elpiclio B.*

"Man! These books are amazing!"
—*Dominique J.*

BLUFORD HIGH

Lost and Found

A Matter of Trust

Secrets in the Shadows

Someone to Love Me

The Bully

Payback

Until We Meet Again

Blood Is Thicker

Brothers in Arms

Summer of Secrets

The Fallen

Shattered

Search for Safety

No Way Out

Schooled

Breaking Point

The Test

Pretty Ugly

Breaking Point

**KARYN LANGHORNE FOLAN
& PAUL LANGAN**

Series Editor: Paul Langan

SCHOLASTIC INC.

ISBN 978-0-545-39551-9

12 11 10 9 8 7 6 5 4 3 2 1   12 13 14 15 16 17/0

Printed in the U.S.A.   23

First Scholastic printing, November 2012

Chapter 1

"You're coming, right?"

For a second, Vicky Fallon wasn't sure if her best friend, Teresa Ortiz, had heard her. Their last class had just ended, and the corridors of Bluford High School were filled with the roar of rushing students and slamming lockers. It was so noisy, Vicky was about to repeat her question when Teresa's dark brown eyes narrowed.

"Coming where?" she asked innocently.

A group of boys jostled by, bumping her. Teresa shot them a mean look. "Watch where you're goin'," she grumbled, shaking her head. Her black hair, pinned up in a loose ponytail, swished against the back of her neck like a mane.

"You know, Martin's hearing!" Vicky said. She'd mentioned the hearing to Teresa earlier but didn't get a clear answer. Now sophomores, she and Teresa had been friends since kindergarten. They had been neighbors until three years ago when Dad moved the family to their little house off Union Street. Some of Vicky's earliest memories were of playing with Teresa. But lately Vicky felt a strange tension between them, especially when Martin Luna's name came up.

"I thought you had to go straight home to help your *abuelo* today," Teresa said. Her voice had an edge to it. A hostile edge Vicky had heard countless times. But it was never aimed at her.

"I do . . . I mean I *did*," Vicky said with a wince. It was true her grandfather was moving into their house this afternoon. Her mother had made the decision after he slipped in his apartment and cracked his hip last month. Mom had even reminded Vicky this morning to come straight home after school to help.

"I'm leaving as soon as the hearing's over. What can I do? Martin needs us to show up for him," Vicky explained, trying to push the image of her grandfather from her mind. Ever since her grandmother died last year, he had been wilting like a tree caught in an endless drought.

"That means you, too, Teresa," Vicky continued. "You read what Martin wrote in English class about his little brother dying. You know Steve and his friends have been ganging up on him just because he's new—"

"That's one version of the story," huffed Teresa.

"Look," Vicky said, rolling her eyes. "I don't know what you've got against him, but—"

"You don't know what I've got against him?" Teresa snapped, her eyes glaring. "Do you even remember what today is?" she demanded.

Vicky shrugged, trying to remember.

"*Great*," Teresa muttered, tossing some books into her backpack. "The fitting for my *quinceañera*? The dresses for *las damas*? For my court? Hello! I can't believe you totally forgot."

Vicky took a deep breath. *Not this again*, she thought.

Teresa's fifteenth birthday was a month away, and lately her party, her *quinceañera,* was all she ever talked about. Her dress, her shoes, her court, which boy from school she would ask to be her escort. Teresa even boasted how her family decided to hire a DJ and arrange a special Mass for her at St. Anna's Church. Vicky knew the tradition. She'd gone to her cousin's *quinceañera* a few years ago. But she also knew Teresa's parents weren't rich. They would have to borrow money to pay for it all.

What a complete waste, she thought.

"Come on, Teresa. We don't have time for this now," she said quickly, eyeing her watch. The hearing was about to start. "Besides, I already told you I couldn't try on dresses today—"

"No, you told me you couldn't come because *your grandfather* was moving in," Teresa shot back. "Now it sounds like you're not coming because of Martin Luna." She crossed her arms in front of her chest. "You've dropped everything because of him!"

"That's not true!" Vicky said angrily, her head beginning to pound. "He's in trouble. You know what I'm saying, Teresa. This is his last chance—"

"Do you even hear yourself? Ever since he came to this school, you've been running around after him like

4

you've never seen a boy before!" Teresa's voice rose as she spoke. Vicky noticed two girls at the end of the hallway staring at them. "It's not like he's even worth it. I mean all he's done since he got here is fight and get into trouble—"

"You know those fights weren't his fault! He never started anything. You know how Steve and Clarence are—"

"Would you wake up, Vicky?" Teresa interrupted, shaking her head so strongly that her ponytail whipped along her neck. "Martin isn't any better. Him getting expelled is probably the best thing for everyone—especially you!"

You're wrong, Vicky wanted to say. *You're totally wrong about him. You don't know him like I do.* But there wasn't time. She needed to go. Now.

"Are you coming or not?" Vicky demanded.

Teresa's eyes flared. She slammed her locker shut and started walking away. Vicky couldn't believe it.

"See you tomorrow, Vicky," she said coolly. "By the way, you owe ninety-five dollars for your dress, whether it fits or not."

"Ninety-five dollars!" Vicky fumed, unable to hide her outrage. "You never said that!"

"Yes I did, but you weren't listening," Teresa grumbled. "You were probably thinking about *Martin* or something," she added, saying his name as if it left a bad taste in her mouth.

Vicky wanted to tell her off right there. She didn't have a single cent to spend on Teresa's party, let alone ninety-five dollars. Where could she get that much money? Certainly not from her parents, who did nothing but argue about money since her dad lost his job at the auto dealership months ago.

"*Whatever*," Vicky muttered. "I can't deal with this right now."

She turned her back on Teresa and hurried away.

Vicky spotted Mr. Mitchell, her English teacher, as she neared the auditorium. He was standing outside the scuffed steel doors in a dark blue suit. A small group of students huddled near him. They looked scared.

"Just in time, Vicky," Mr. Mitchell said with a smile. "Are you ready?" he asked.

"I guess so," she said, grateful that he had decided to help defend Martin. She glanced into the auditorium. In the distance, she could see Martin and a woman who must be his mother, her olive face lined with worry. Looking at them, Vicky's stomach sank. She had never spoken at a hearing before and wondered if she had made a mistake by agreeing to now.

"Kinda scary, huh?" said Eric Acosta, the freshman Martin defended in his last fight at Bluford. After Martin got in trouble, Vicky had asked Eric to help her gather people to support him at his hearing. Eric bravely agreed to help, but now he looked nervous, fidgeting with the zipper of his backpack as he looked at her.

"Yeah, a little," she mumbled, her mouth suddenly dry. Nearby, Vicky saw Roylin Bailey, a junior who failed English last year and was now in her class. He leaned against the wall with his arms crossed on his chest, his loud mouth unusually silent. A small group of boys from Eric's gym class were there too, as well as two boys from the freshman football team. They looked tense, like witnesses before a trial. She knew some students at Bluford considered them snitches for being willing to speak up to the superintendent. But what choice did they have? If they kept silent,

Martin would be kicked out unfairly. Allowing that was worse than being a snitch, Vicky figured.

"Well, I think this is everyone," said Mr. Mitchell, taking a second to look at each of them. "Your presence at this hearing is important. No matter what happens, I'm proud of you for standing up for what you believe in. And I am proud of you, Vicky, for getting everybody together."

"Thanks," Vicky muttered, cringing at Mr. Mitchell's ominous words.

No matter what happens.

She still couldn't believe that Martin Luna was about to get expelled. It felt as if he was being stolen from her somehow. It wasn't right.

Sure, Martin had been in a few fights since he transferred to Bluford. But that was because Vicky's ex-boyfriend, Steve Morris, started with him. Yes, Martin had shoved a teacher, but that was an accident. He was just trying to protect Eric. Yes, Martin walked Bluford's halls with a swagger, but he also had the darkest, most intense eyes Vicky had ever seen. Eyes that pulled her like a magnet whenever she looked into them.

"All right, everyone. It's time. Let's

go," Mr. Mitchell said. He quickly led them into the auditorium. Gray metal chairs were arranged in neat rows on the speckled tile floor. From behind, they looked like gravestones in a sea of dusty cardboard.

Vicky felt her stomach tremble. Her mind raced with questions.

What if Martin is kicked out?

Would he be sent to juvenile hall?

Is this the end for us?

Just a few days ago she'd stood with Martin, alone in the small apartment he shared with his mother. That was when he told her how Huero, his eight-year-old brother, had been killed in a drive-by shooting last July. Martin's eyes glistened with tears as he showed her pictures of him. She could still hear how Martin's voice shook as he described how Huero died in his arms, the blood dripping through his fingers.

"*It should have been me,*" Martin had confessed, leaning into her.

In that moment, she felt the weight of his body, the rhythmic thump of his heart. All his anger and swagger were gone. Instead, Martin cried and she held him, touched his face, felt the pain gush from him in waves. She had never been so close to a boy, not even with Steve Morris, her ex-boyfriend. It was as if they were the only two people in the world. As if she had reached in and touched his soul somehow.

And then it happened. She kissed him, tasting his tears as if they were her own. Though it was days ago, she hadn't told anyone about what happened. Not her mother who was too stressed lately to listen. Not her father who seemed to care more about watching football than anything else since he lost his job. Not even Teresa. Vicky knew she'd only roll her eyes.

"Okay, the hearing's about to start," Mr. Mitchell whispered, interrupting Vicky's thoughts. "That's Mr. Gates up there. He's the superintendent," he said, nodding toward an older white man who sat at the end of a long table. The man held a thick folder and glared down at Martin as if he was annoyed at him.

"*Great*," Vicky mumbled to herself.

Ms. Spencer, Bluford's principal, sat at the other end of the table. Martin and his mother were in chairs in the front row. Martin's face was pale, his jaw tense. She knew he was scared. She wished she could get up and sit next to him.

"When it's your turn," Mr. Mitchell advised, "remember not to excuse Martin's behavior. We all know what he did was wrong. We just want Mr. Gates to understand that there are reasons for Martin's behavior and that expelling him isn't the solution. Understand?"

Vicky nodded as Mr. Gates cleared his throat and read a long list of disciplinary problems. Each was a charge against Martin.

Fights. Cutting school. Skipping classes. Hitting a teacher. The list seemed to go on and on. Vicky wondered if Martin even had a chance.

"Well, Mr. Luna, what do you have to say for yourself?" Mr. Gates asked when he had finished reading. "Why do you think you should be allowed to stay at Bluford High?"

Martin stood up nervously. Vicky's heart pounded. She leaned forward in her chair waiting for him to speak. Behind her someone coughed. The air in the auditorium suddenly felt thick and heavy. Martin stammered.

"C'mon! Say something!" she wanted to scream.

Seconds ticked by. Martin seemed overwhelmed and unsure of himself.

11

Vicky was in agony.

"Fight for yourself!" she almost shouted the words in the middle of the auditorium. If he didn't explain himself, Vicky knew her help would be useless. He would be expelled in a few minutes.

"C'mon!"

Finally, Martin broke his silence.

"I'm sorry about what happened the other day. I never meant to hurt no one. Things in this school are a little different from where I come from," Martin began. He then described the events of the past year, including the day his brother got shot and died in his arms.

The auditorium grew silent except for the sound of his voice. Vicky cringed at the sad details and winced when Martin admitted he had been so angry he wanted to kill his brother's shooter. Mr. Gates didn't even blink as he spoke.

But then Martin told the story about how he had changed from that path. He admitted his mistakes and described how people at Bluford had helped him, including Mr. Mitchell.

"Maybe if I never came to this school, I'd have thrown my life away. But being here gave me a chance to think and see another way," he said glancing at the

12

crowd. "And more than anything, I have to live a better life for my little brother. I gotta live the future he'll never have," he confessed, his voice heavy with emotion. "That's what I hope to do right here at Bluford."

A hush gripped the auditorium. Even the janitors had stopped working to listen. It was as if everyone was stunned by what they heard.

"*See, I told you he wasn't bad*," Vicky wanted to shout to anyone who would listen.

Mr. Gates cleared his throat. "Does anyone else have anything to add on this matter?" he asked.

Mr. Mitchell stood up. Vicky joined him, her palms sweaty and her knees shaking. This was her chance to help. But as Mr. Mitchell explained why they were there, Mr. Gates smiled and silenced him with words that thundered through the auditorium.

"I don't think expulsion is necessary at this point . . ."

Vicky's jaw dropped and then she heard herself cheering. Mr. Mitchell and others clapped loudly as Martin hugged his mother. Vicky rushed forward, unable to stop herself.

"Oh my God, Martin. You did it!" she cried, embracing him. "I'm so happy for you!"

"Thanks, Vicky," Martin said as tears rolled down his cheeks. "Thanks for being here."

Vicky wiped her eyes and hugged him once more, surprised at her own feelings. She was thrilled for him but also happy for herself. She would get to see him again. What they started could continue. It was a dream come true.

"I can't stay," she told him. "I promised my mom I'd be home a half-hour ago." She tried to smile. "I'm probably in big trouble."

"Go," Martin told her, though she could tell by the look on his face that he really wanted her to stay. "I'll talk to you later?"

Vicky nodded. "Yes, definitely. Congratulations, Martin," she said, forcing herself away from him.

She glanced over her shoulder one last time before leaving the auditorium. Martin was shaking hands with Mr. Mitchell, but his eyes were on her.

Chapter 2

Vicky raced down the halls, rushing past the metal detectors, out the main doorway, down the concrete steps, and away from the school. She hurried by the SuperFoods parking lot where Martin and Frankie clashed a few weeks earlier. She ignored the new graffiti on the store's stucco walls, the flies that buzzed on a trash bag left on the sidewalk, the cars that passed by with their rumbling sound systems that filled the air with bass, their drivers staring at her body as if her face didn't exist. She had no time for any of it.

Please let me get there before Mom, Vicky hoped, turning the corner to her block.

But as she neared her house, she spotted her mother's black Civic, the car

Dad bought a few months before he lost his job. It was already parked in the driveway. The trunk was open, and Vicky could see that it was full of boxes. More were stacked in the backseat. She was too late.

Vicky reached the driveway just as Danny, her little brother, stepped out the front door. He was a seventh grader at Irving Middle School. He flashed her a look as he headed to the car.

"It's about time," he grumbled. "Did you forget Abuelo's moving in today?"

"No, I didn't *forget*," Vicky snapped. "I just had something I needed to do."

"Like what?" he asked, lifting a stack of boxes from the trunk.

"None of your business." She knew better than to explain Martin's hearing to her little brother. He couldn't keep a secret, and she didn't want him blurting Martin's name to Mom and Dad, especially not now. "I just got held up at school, that's all."

"Yeah, well, Mom's mad," he said, heading into the house.

Great, Vicky thought as she grabbed a box and followed him.

Inside, the normally neat living room was cluttered with stuffed trash bags and musty old suitcases. Vicky stepped carefully around the piles and dropped her backpack on the sofa. Her pillow and blankets were stacked on the far end of the couch. Now that Abuelo had arrived, she was going to be sleeping in the living room. They had decided this because Abuelo was unsteady on his feet and needed to be near a bathroom. Vicky's room was closest, just across the hall.

At first, Danny had volunteered to sleep on the couch and give Vicky his room but Mom refused.

"No, mijo. You have enough trouble staying focused on school right now. I'm not gonna have you losing sleep watching TV or playing video games all night. Forget it," she had said.

Dad also offered to sleep in the living room but Vicky disagreed. She didn't want to be the reason her parents were apart, not with how they had been acting lately. Besides, she'd rather sleep alone on the couch than share a bed with Mom, who talked in her sleep.

But looking at the cluttered living room, Vicky wondered if she had made a mistake. Even after the boxes were emptied and stored away, she knew there would be no privacy, no place to get away from her brother or escape her parents' arguments. Nowhere to go when she wanted to talk to Martin.

"Vicky!" Mom's voice cut through her thoughts like an axe. "Is that you?"

Vicky braced herself. "Yeah," she said, rushing down the hall.

"Where have you been?" Mom barked. She stepped out of the bedroom. Her dark hair was sweaty and clung to her forehead and cheeks. Her eyes glared.

Vicky knew not to mention Martin, not when Mom was this angry.

"Teresa needed me to help—"

"Teresa!" Mom fumed as if she'd just been insulted. "I told you this was important, Vicky. We needed you here! Your father didn't show up either."

"I'm sorry—"

"Danny and I had to load everything by ourselves. We're lucky Abuelo didn't slip and fall again," she grumbled, rubbing her temples as if her head hurt.

"I'm sorry. It's just that—"

"I don't want to hear it, Vicky. Get in there and help Danny. And say hello to your grandfather."

Vicky peered into her room and nearly gasped at the frail man sitting on the edge of her bed. He looked as if he had aged years since Grandma's funeral last September. When Vicky was a little girl, Abuelo always seemed so strong and healthy. Now he was a shriveled version of himself. She could tell he had lost weight, too. His flannel shirt hung loosely from his neck and his cheeks were hollow and a bit sunken. His gnarled fingers, which once could fix almost anything, now rested on the aluminum walker that sat in front of him.

"*Hola, niña*," he said with a weak smile. For an instant, his eyes brightened, and Vicky saw a flash of the man she remembered.

"Hello, Abuelo." She leaned over and kissed his cheek. His skin felt like old newspaper. "I'm sorry I'm late. I had something important to finish at school."

Abuelo shook his head, as if he didn't want her to apologize. Then he reached out to her. Vicky wasn't sure if he wanted to pat her hair or her face, but either way, his hand missed and brushed the air beside her head. "I'm sorry about your room," he said in Spanish.

"*De nada*," Vicky mumbled, feeling a bit self-conscious about her Spanish.

Dad was mostly Irish. Born in Pittsburgh, he never learned to speak more than a few words of Spanish, so they rarely used it at home. Vicky understood it from listening to neighbors and relatives, but speaking it properly to her grandfather was another matter.

"Don't worry, *Papi*. We have enough room. She'll be fine," Mom said then, her voice still tinged with anger. She turned back to Vicky. "Put those shirts away and break up those boxes," she ordered, pointing to a pile of shirts at the foot of her bed.

Vicky grabbed the clothing and opened her closet door. She was surprised to see it was empty. Her clothes were gone.

"Where are my things?" she asked before she could stop herself.

"I had to put them in Danny's room," her mother replied. "He had the most extra space."

"Oh," Vicky replied, feeling a wave of anger spread through her chest.

Couldn't you just ask me first? Couldn't you leave some of my stuff where it belongs? Did you have to put it all in his *room?* she wanted to say. But Abuelo was next to her. She didn't want to hurt his feelings, and she could tell by the way Mom's lips were pressed together that complaining wouldn't help.

Vicky hung the shirts without a word. Then she helped Danny move the rest of Abuelo's boxes to her room. Mom put Univision on the living room TV so Abuelo would stay there and watch it. But he insisted on sitting in the bedroom with them.

"I should help," he said several times. Once, he even tried to get up, grunting with effort, but his legs were wobbly and unsteady. The doctors said he would be this way for weeks, maybe longer.

"No, Papi. You just relax," Mom ordered. Vicky caught her mother staring at Abuelo when he wasn't looking. Her eyes were puffy and red, as if she was crying invisible tears.

"That's the last one, Mom," Danny announced, gently dropping two more big boxes on the floor by Vicky's bed. "The car's empty and everything from the living room is in here now."

"Good," her mother said with a weak smile as she patted Danny's back. "Thanks, *mijo*."

Just then, Vicky heard the front door

open and then slam shut. It was followed seconds later by the dull jingle of keys and the familiar thud of footsteps. It was Dad. Almost immediately, the TV switched from Spanish to English. Vicky knew what was coming next. *Sports.* Lately that was Dad's obsession. Especially college football. Penn State.

Mom's jaw tightened as the sound of the TV grew louder. Dad had turned it up.

"Be right back," Mom huffed. Vicky knew her mother was trying to sound calm, but the way she marched out and shut the door said otherwise. Vicky braced herself.

Not again, Vicky thought. *Not another fight.* Danny shook his head heavily. The TV cut off abruptly.

"Where have you been?! You promised you'd meet me at my father's at 3:00!" Mom yelled. Her voice pierced the thin walls as if they were cardboard. "If you've been down at that sports bar—"

"I've been all over town looking for work, so just lay off of me, Yolanda, okay?" Dad snapped. "I musta driven fifty miles today and spent two hours stuck in traffic for nothing. And now I come in only to have you jumping down my throat like I'm some kind of—"

"Shh!" Mom hissed. "Lower your voice. I won't have you screaming in this house while my father is here."

"It's *my* house too—"

"Yeah, well, act like it! Right now it seems like the only one keeping everything together around here is me!"

"You think I'm not trying? What do you think I been doin' all day?"

"I don't know what you were doin', Michael. But you weren't here when I needed you. And now that you're here, all you're doing is watching TV and feeling sorry for yourself," Mom yelled.

"Yolanda—"

"No, don't *Yolanda* me," Mom snapped. "I been running around all day, too! But I don't have time to rest. You don't see me watching TV! You may be writin' the checks, Michael, but where you think the money is coming from?" Mom's job as a Transit Authority secretary was keeping them afloat since Dad lost his job.

"I know, I know," Dad said wearily. "I'm trying."

"Well try *harder*," Mom barked. "And next time, if you promise me you'll be here, then be here."

Vicky heard her mother stomp into the

kitchen. Soon pots and pans were rattling as if she was taking out her anger on them. Vicky's stomach churned. Lately, they were fighting all the time. Usually, Vicky would retreat to her room to get away, but now that was impossible. Next to her, Danny bundled a trash bag, his jaw clenched with tension.

Abuelo grunted. "It's okay," he said, rubbing her shoulder with a shaky hand. "Your grandmother used to yell at me all the time. Don't worry."

"Yeah, well, that's all they ever do anymore," said Danny.

"Relax. Mom's just tired, that's all," Vicky replied, only half believing her words. "We better break the rest of those boxes down," she added, getting up from the bed—anything to change the subject. She leaned forward to help, and her necklace swung from beneath her shirt. Hanging from it was the silver and turquoise cross that once belonged to her grandmother.

Abuelo's eyes suddenly focused. "*Ay Dios mio!* You still wear her cross?" he asked.

Vicky clutched the chain and nodded. "Always."

A crinkled smile spread across

Abuelo's face. "She got that for her *quinceañera*. I was there. We were your age then. So long ago," he said wistfully, his eyes glistening. "Don't lose it. As long as you have it, she's with you."

Suddenly, the bedroom door opened and her parents appeared in the doorway.

"Look, Papi," Mom said in a voice that sounded both very sweet and very fake. "Michael's home."

"Welcome, Diego," Dad said, reaching out his hand to Abuelo. "Good to see you again."

Vicky couldn't help but notice that her father looked drained. Black stubble covered the lower half of his face. Saggy creases, the beginnings of wrinkles, stretched from the corners of his mouth. Even his shirt and tie looked limp. Before the dealership closed, Dad always looked good—neatly pressed shirts, a hint of cologne, always a wide smile and a joke. He had worked long hours, but he had always been happy and full of life. Now he seemed defeated.

Please, let him get another job soon, Vicky prayed in her mind. *Please.*

"These two making you comfortable?" her father added, as if the question required all his effort.

"*Si*," her grandfather answered, then continued in English. "Yes. Thank you for having me in your home, Michael."

Vicky's father nodded again. "Well, if everything is under control here, I could use a shower—"

Ring!

Vicky cringed at the sound of the phone. *Here we go again*, she thought.

For the past month or two, the phone was constantly ringing, especially at dinnertime. Vicky knew the calls were from bill collectors. She had heard the messages, though her parents never actually discussed them with her. They didn't need to.

Her father flashed Mom a quick glance and shook his head. "I got it," he muttered, walking down the hallway. He looked as if he was going to his own hanging.

"Vicky, when you're finished here, I could use some help with dinner," Mom said quickly. She knew Mom was trying to distract her from Dad's conversation.

"It's for you, Vicky," her father said then, sounding relieved. "Some boy, Martin."

Martin!

Vicky felt her cheeks flush. She dashed out of the bedroom and grabbed the phone from her father. She paused, expecting him to stand nearby and listen, the way he did when Steve used to call. But instead Dad went to the front door and grabbed the mail. She watched him flip through the pile and pull out a thick white envelope. He tore it open and scanned the page inside quickly, cursing under his breath. He then jammed it deep into his pocket and stormed to his bedroom. Finally, she was free.

"Hello," she said, once his door was closed.

"Hey girl, wassup?" Martin asked, his voice hoarse, as if he had been talking for hours. "I wanted to thank you again for what you did today."

"I didn't do anything," Vicky said, remembering the hearing. It already seemed like days had passed since then. "*You* did it. You were really great, Martin. I'm so proud of you."

"Thanks, Vic. But it never would have happened if it hadn't been for you. You talked me into it—into fighting to stay in school. I still can't believe it," Martin confessed. "Without you, I woulda just accepted whatever they said, you know?"

"That wasn't gonna happen. I wouldn't let them kick you out," she said.

"Girl, you're crazy! When I saw you ready to stand up for me like that . . ." Martin's voice cracked with emotion. She had heard the sound before, the afternoon they were alone in his apartment. "I still can't believe it. Like I said, thank you. You're the closest . . . friend I got."

"Is that what we are now, friends?" Vicky teased, her heart racing. She wished she could reach through the phone and touch his face. She knew they were more than just friends, though they hadn't actually said it. Not yet.

"Who you talking to?" a voice interrupted. Vicky looked up to see Danny eyeing her curiously, a smirk on his face. "He the reason you were late today?"

"Boy, mind your own business," she said, turning her back on him to hide her smile.

"Who's that?" Martin asked.

"My little brother," Vicky replied, thinking about how Martin might react to those words after all he had been through. "He's in seventh grade," she added quickly to fill the silence. "But most of the time, he acts like a third grader—"

"Vicky, I need your help with dinner," Mom hollered from the kitchen.

"One minute!" Vicky yelled back, rolling her eyes. It was the first nice moment she'd had since she got home, and already Mom was ruining it.

"I gotta go, Martin," she huffed.

"Okay," he said, hesitating for a second. "Hey, if you're free tomorrow, maybe you could meet me after school. We could chill at Niko's Pizza or go to the park or something. I really want to talk to you about a bunch of things."

Vicky's heart fluttered again. She wished she was with Martin right now, not stuck in the house with her angry parents, her sad grandfather, and her nosy brother. "I'd like that too," she said, her face burning with excitement.

"Cool. I guess I'll see you then."

"Definitely."

"*Vicky!*" Mom yelled again, shattering their conversation. "I need you. *Now!*"

"All right!" Vicky shouted back, reluctantly hanging up the phone.

She clung to Martin's words hours later as she lay sleepless on the sofa. In the gloom, she could hear angry voices.

Her parents were still fighting.

At 3:27 a.m. Vicky awoke to a strange blue light. She opened her eyes to see her father sitting motionless in front of the TV. His eyes were glazed and unblinking, his face ghostly in the eerie glow. Slow motion highlights of a football game flickered on the screen in front of him.

"Dad?" she asked.

He jumped as if he had been shocked. Quickly he rose from his chair.

"Go back to sleep, princess. It's late," he said, snapping the TV off. Without a word, he draped an extra blanket over her, gave her a kiss, and disappeared in the dark hallway.

When she woke up hours later, she wondered if it had all been a dream. But then she spotted the heavy blanket on her legs and knew it was real.

Too real.

Chapter 3

"So . . ." Mr. Mitchell said with a playful grin as he scanned the crowded classroom. "What's wrong with Ophelia?"

The class groaned. The bell had barely rung before Mr. Mitchell was pacing the room like a boxer. As usual, he was excited to talk about their English homework, Act III of Shakespeare's *Hamlet*.

"Here we go again," someone mumbled.

"Maybe Ophelia got too much homework," joked Roylin Bailey from the back of the room.

"At least she *does* hers," snapped Steve Morris with a smirk.

Roylin scowled.

"I think her problems go a bit deeper than homework, gentlemen," Mr. Mitchell cut in.

Vicky fought back a yawn. She had read Act II days ago but could barely remember it. Her head was foggy and her back sore from the long night on the couch. Now that Martin's hearing was over, she'd hoped to arrive early and maybe smooth things out with Teresa. But after being up for hours listening to her parents fighting, Vicky was late to class.

Teresa was already seated, her eyes glued to a page of her notebook when Vicky arrived. Vicky waited for her to look up or say hi, but Teresa didn't budge. Instead, she acted as if Vicky wasn't there.

Who are you kidding, Teresa? Vicky wanted to say. *We both know you don't care that much about schoolwork.* After a minute of Teresa's icy silence, Vicky gave up.

"Fine. Be that way," she mumbled loud enough for Teresa to hear.

Martin had snuck into class as the bell rang. He had flashed her a quick smile just as Mr. Mitchell started his lecture.

"Seriously," Mr. Mitchell continued, pausing at Teresa's desk. "Pretend Ophelia's your best friend. Think about how Hamlet and her father are treating her. What advice would you give her? Let's start with you, Teresa."

For a second, Teresa was quiet. Then a funny look spread over her face and she glanced over at Vicky. "Well, for one thing, I'd tell her she's got boy troubles," Teresa joked. "But don't we all?"

The class snickered. Normally Vicky would have laughed, too. But something about Teresa's comment was sharp, like a dart aimed at her.

"Okay. Good!" Mr. Mitchell nodded, stepping to the front of the room and writing Teresa's words on the chalkboard. Vicky noticed that he wore a maroon tie with a picture of balding man with a funny mustache and a ruffled collar. Underneath the picture, the word "Shakespeare" was written in fancy gold script. "Tell me more, Teresa. What do you mean by *boy troubles*?"

"Well, Hamlet is no good. One minute he tells her he likes her, but then he acts like he's not interested. If she was my friend, I'd tell her to drop him." Again Teresa flashed Vicky a smug look. It was as if she was talking about Martin, not Hamlet.

"Well, I think you'd just make her

problems worse," cut in Martin.

Several students turned in surprise. Martin seemed to ignore them. His dark eyes focused on Teresa, almost as if he was challenging her.

"Oh snap!" Roylin said, seeming to enjoy the disagreement.

Vicky felt her stomach sink. Couldn't they just get along?

"What do you mean, Martin? Explain," said Mr. Mitchell.

"I mean she just needs her space, that's all. Ophelia's problem is everyone's all up in her business. Her dad says one thing. Her brother tells her something else. Hamlet keeps telling her what to do. She don't need more advice. She just needs everyone to back off and let her figure out what she's doing."

"No disrespect, but I'm glad you're not giving me advice, bro," said another voice.

Vicky cringed. It was Steve Morris. He leaned forward in his seat, his broad shoulders stretching his Bluford Football T-shirt tight across his back. He looked as if he was about to pounce. Vicky had seen it all before.

"Why, Steve?" Mr. Mitchell asked.

"I just think Martin's wrong. Yeah,

Ophelia's gettin' too much advice. But that don't mean the advice is bad. Straight up, if your friend's makin' a mistake, you gotta tell her, even if she don't wanna hear it. Whether it's Shakespeare or real life, you gotta tell it like it is—just like Teresa said," Steve explained.

As he finished, his eyes locked on Vicky's. For a second, the classroom grew silent. Vicky felt Teresa staring at her too, along with several other students. Suddenly it was as if an invisible spotlight was shining on her. Somehow she, not Ophelia, had become the topic of discussion. She squirmed in her chair.

"An excellent discussion. And to think, this play is about four hundred years old and still has something to say," Mr. Mitchell said, looking back at Vicky. Was he studying her, too? Her face grew hot under his gaze. "You have something you want to add, Vicky?" he asked.

Nothing I can say here, she thought to herself. She shook her head and watched as Mr. Mitchell turned away and circled to the other side of the room.

"Pay attention to Ophelia as you read

Act IV for homework," he added. "She's under a lot of pressure. What happens to her may surprise you." He moved to the chalkboard and began writing terms on the board.

Foreshadowing
Imagery
Metaphor

Vicky's mind wandered as his hands scuffed along the chalkboard. She couldn't wait for the school day to end so she could get out of Bluford. Then she could be alone with Martin. Maybe they would go to the park and stroll hand in hand the way they did weeks ago. Maybe they would even kiss again. The thought made her heart race.

Martin's soft lips. The electricity in her body. Her heart pounding . . .

The only other boy she had really kissed was Steve Morris. His mouth was always too firm, and his cologne so strong that it made her eyes water. She had even told Teresa about it.

"Oh my God, for real?" Teresa had squealed. *"But he's got the best body in our whole class."*

It was true that Steve's body was amazing, like a sculpture or a magazine ad. Once, she had seen him shirtless after a football game and found herself blushing at his stomach muscles. Other girls noticed him too. She had heard the talk all over Bluford High School.

Steve, the star running back.

Steve, the athlete who was going to get a football scholarship.

Steve the hero who scored the winning touchdown against Lincoln High.

Vicky was sick of hearing about it. She remembered a different Steve Morris, the chubby fifth grader who used to be in her class at St. Gabriel's School. That was the year his parents divorced. She could still picture him crying in Principal Worrell's office. A bunch of eighth graders teased him because his Dad stopped coming to his football games.

"Where's your pops? He get tired of watching you fumble?"

"Nah, he couldn't fit in the car no more, 'cause Steve's so big."

"If my boy was that fat, I'd leave home too."

Steve had snapped, flailing at them, tears in his eyes. The boys laughed, shoving him back each time he lunged at them. Vicky had to grab a teacher to stop Steve from getting beat up.

Afterward, he got expelled and went to public school. Three years later, when her parents could no longer afford Catholic school, Vicky transferred to Irving Middle School and found Steve again. By then, he had grown bigger and become an athlete. Kids no longer teased him. But Vicky was surprised to see that he acted just like the boys who used to hassle him. He had become something of a bully.

Yet sometimes Vicky still saw flashes of the sad boy in Steve's eyes, the person he was before his father broke his heart and filled him with anger, before girls started treating him as if he could do no wrong, before colleges began scouting him and telling him he was special. That's why she agreed to go with him to the Spring Formal last year. But he had spent most of the night with his buddies mocking a group of freshman boys who seemed too scared to dance.

"Why do you act that way?" Vicky had said after the dance was over.

"What way?"

"You know what I mean. Teasing kids who aren't bothering you. Why do you do that?"

"I don't know," he admitted, shrugging

his thick shoulders. *"Sometimes it's like I can't help it, you know? Like I see them and I just get angry."*

"Maybe 'cause you used to be like that?" she challenged. "I remember, Steve. I was there. I can't believe you'd act that way after all you been through."

"Please!" he fumed. *"If I was still like them scared kids, would you be at this dance with me?"*

"Yeah," Vicky said. "I would."

"Yeah right," Steve huffed. *"The old me is gone, Vic. People used to laugh at me, but that don't happen no more. People stopped laughing 'cause they know sooner or later I'm gonna beat 'em. And that's what I do. Maybe you don't like it, but that's the way it is."*

Vicky knew he was being honest, but his words made her wince. It was as if something inside him was broken. As if what happened in middle school had forever changed him. It turned everything into a competition. It made him a great athlete, but it also made him mean. And whenever Vicky watched him, no matter how beautiful his body, she saw something else when he acted this way. Ugliness. Teresa couldn't understand.

"You're crazy. You know how many girls wanna get with him?" she said.

"They can have him," Vicky had replied.

Martin was totally different. Vicky knew he had been hurt too, that there was a sea of rage inside him. But underneath it all was something Steve didn't have. A part she heard in Martin's soft voice, read in his words about Huero, and saw in his sad eyes. A part that made her want to be closer to him.

"Hello?"

Vicky nearly jumped out of her seat. Mr. Mitchell was standing next to her, leaning over her desk.

"Vicky? Did you hear me?"

Vicky looked around in embarrassment. She had no idea what they were talking about. She had been completely lost in her own thoughts. Everyone was staring at her.

"Where you at, girl?" Roylin said. Laughter erupted around her, and her face suddenly burned.

"I'm s-sorry, Mr. Mitchell," she stammered. "I didn't hear the question."

Mr. Mitchell glanced at her notebook. Vicky tried to cover up the little sketches she had made during class. But she knew he could see some of them: little drawings of hearts with her initials and Martin's in the center. He stepped back slightly, as if he was surprised.

"The question was—"

RING!

The bell blared overhead. Mr. Mitchell sighed and stepped away from Vicky's desk.

Thank God, Vicky thought. All around her, chairs scraped as people rushed to the door. Teresa stood up without a word, though her expression changed. Instead of anger, she almost looked confused. Maybe a bit concerned, too.

But before she could speak, Martin stepped in between them, smiling at Vicky. His eyes never seemed more intense. Teresa must have noticed. She bolted into the hallway as if she had seen something that disgusted her.

"Hi," he said softly.

Vicky felt a warm blush spread across her face. For a second, she didn't know what to say. Her mind was blank. All the troubles at home, the drama with Teresa, and even the embarrassment of class melted away. Lost in a foggy haze.

"Hey," she said. "I can't believe what just happened. I completely zoned out."

"Nah, you were just giving someone else a chance to answer the questions for a change," he replied. "You can't always be the one with all the answers."

"Yeah, well, if I don't start getting some sleep soon, you're gonna have to answer them for me."

"How come you didn't sleep?"

Vicky took a deep breath. "That's a long story," she said, unsure whether to tell him her parents were fighting.

"Excuse me. Don't you two have a class to go to?"

Vicky turned to see Mr. Mitchell. She had totally forgotten about him—again.

Martin nodded. "Yes, sir. Sorry," he said, leading her toward the door. "Come on."

In the hallway, Vicky spotted Teresa at her locker. She flipped through her back-pack as if she was looking for something. Vicky was sure she was just stalling.

"So . . . I'll see you after school?" Martin asked.

"I can't wait," Vicky said. "Meet me right here."

"Cool," Martin said, pausing awkwardly as if he was waiting for something. Vicky wanted to talk to him, but she could feel Teresa listening to every word. Martin seemed to understand. He glanced down at Teresa for a moment with a smirk on his face. Then he shook his head and walked away. Vicky watched him go, wishing the day was over.

Crash!

Teresa slammed her locker shut and walked right up to her.

Vicky stared straight through her old friend. "*What?*" she asked.

"You tell me," Teresa replied. "You seemed so out of it today. I know it's 'cause of Martin—"

"You don't know anything!" Vicky snapped, anger flaring in her chest. "And if all you're gonna do is dog him, I don't have anything to say to you!"

"Just calm down, okay. I'm not going to lie and pretend I like him—"

"*Teresa*—"

"Just listen to me, okay? I heard about the hearing yesterday, and I wanted to tell you I spoke to my mom about Martin."

"*Huh?*"

Teresa took a deep breath as if she was about to make a difficult announcement. "It's okay if you want to bring him to my *quinceañera*," Teresa explained.

Vicky sighed. *The quinceañera. Again.*

That's what this was all about.

"He knows what to wear, right?" Teresa asked.

Vicky's pulse began to pound. After everything that happened with her parents and at home, Teresa's party was the last thing she wanted to think about.

"He can be a *chamberlan* if he comes with you. But he can't bring any of his friends. My mom don't want no *cholos* there." As she spoke, Teresa wrinkled her nose as if she smelled something bad.

"And no fighting," she added, reaching into the tiny leopard print purse that dangled from her wrist. "Here. This one is yours." She handed Vicky a folded piece of paper.

"What's this?"

Teresa rolled her eyes as if Vicky asked a stupid question. "Girl, what is wrong with you? It's like you're a zombie or something. *It's the bill!* For your dress, remember? We need the money by Friday. Or at least half of it, if you can't get it all."

Vicky clutched the envelope in her fist without looking at it. "I'll be glad when this party is over," she muttered.

"What?"

"You heard me," Vicky fumed, unable to hide her frustration. "All you care about is your *quinceañera*. You said *I'm* out of it. Well, listen to yourself. You act like the whole world revolves around your party."

"What are you so upset about?" Teresa asked. "Is it 'cause you're still jealous? If so, that's your problem, not mine."

"*Jealous?*" Vicky's temples began to throb.

"You know, 'cause all you got for your birthday was some flowers and a cake? I remember what you said."

Teresa's words hit like a slap in the face. It was true her own fifteenth birthday had been little more than a few friends and relatives over for dinner. Vicky had told her parents it didn't matter—that she didn't want a big party—but that was because she knew money was tight. Afterward, she had admitted her disappointment to Teresa. Now Teresa was throwing that secret right back at her. Vicky couldn't believe it.

"You know something, Teresa?" she growled, her fingers tingling with anger. "I wouldn't come to your stupid *quinceañera* if you paid me to go. Here,

45

this one is yours," she added, crumpling the bill and tossing it at Teresa's feet.

Teresa's jaw dropped, but Vicky didn't care. She stormed away, leaving her old friend alone in the emptying hallway.

Chapter 4

"Ms. Fallon, you need to go to the office."

"*Huh?*" Vicky said, startled by Ms. Ford's announcement

She had been daydreaming through geometry, pretending to listen to Ms. Ford's lesson on congruent triangles. She had hardly noticed the office aide come into the classroom and whisper something in her teacher's ear.

"*The office*, Ms. Fallon. The secretary wants you there right now."

"Why? What'd I do?" Vicky said as she got up from her desk. The day was almost over, just one more class to go.

"Oooh, girl, you got busted," joked Shanetta Greene from two rows back.

"Yeah, right. Like *she'd* do anything wrong," teased Roslyn Webb.

Vicky felt her classmates watching as she stepped into the quiet hallway. In all her years of school, she had been called to the office only once. That was the day her grandmother died suddenly of a massive heart attack. The memory made her shudder as she rushed to the office.

What if something happened at home? Is it Abuelo?

"Hi honey," said Ms. Bader, the school secretary, as soon as Vicky arrived. "You have a message. Your mom called. She needs you to go straight home after school today."

"What for?" Vicky asked. "Is something wrong?"

"No, no," Ms. Bader said with a reassuring smile. "She just needs you to stay with your grandfather until she gets home from work."

For a second, Vicky was relieved, but then it hit her what Mom was asking.

What about Martin? I'm supposed to meet him after school, she wanted to say.

"So nice that you spend time with your grandfather," Ms. Bader added. "When I was your age, my grandfather was my best friend."

Vicky wanted to scream.

No, not today! She almost yelled the

48

words. *Why can't Dad do it? Or Danny? It's not fair!*

She knew Abuelo couldn't be alone for long, but after the night on the couch, the embarrassing moment in Mr. Mitchell's class, and the fight with Teresa, the one thing she looked forward to was her time with Martin. And now that was being taken away.

Vicky felt like a blister about to explode.

"Are you feeling okay?" Ms. Bader asked.

Vicky scowled at the old woman. "Yeah, I'm fine," she grumbled, wishing everyone would just disappear.

Vicky stormed to her locker after the final bell. She had hoped to explain things to Martin and leave without seeing Teresa. Just the thought of her made Vicky's eyes twitch.

"Man, what's your problem with her?" said a deep husky voice. "Don't you remember, *she's* the one that ratted you out? You heard what happened in Luna's hearing. Why don't you just forget about both of them? They ain't worth it."

Vicky turned to see Clarence, a huge lineman from Bluford's football team. He always had Steve's back, especially in his fights with Martin. Clarence was talking to Steve Morris. The two were coming down the hallway toward her.

"Boy, I don't need your permission to talk to her. You just don't get it, Clarence. Me and Vicky go way back," Steve said, glancing at her. "Look, I'll catch up with you at practice. Later," he said, bumping fists with his teammate. Clarence looked puzzled as he walked by, leaving Steve alone in front of her locker.

Vicky scanned the bustling hallway for Martin. He was nowhere in sight.

"What do you want?" she sighed.

"C'mon, Vic," Steve scoffed, shaking his head as if he was insulted. His black hair, coiled in tight cornrows, danced on his shoulders. "Why you gotta be like that?"

"Be like what? I shouldn't even be talking to you, not after everything you did to Martin," she said.

Steve rolled his eyes. "Look, I know you're all into him now, but you gotta wake up, girl. Since you're not talking to Teresa, I figure you'd talk to me."

"Huh?"

"Teresa told me y'all are fightin'—"

"I can't believe she's talking about

me to *you!*" Vicky said, feeling her head throb with anger. "Who does she think she is?"

"Calm down," Steve said. "This ain't about her. It's about *you.* She's worried. You ain't been right since Martin started coming 'round—"

"Don't *you* start with me, Steve! You don't know what you're talking about."

"Girl, why you gettin' so upset? Back in the day, I remember you sticking up for me. Maybe you don't remember it, but I do. I'm just trying to return the favor."

"I don't need your help, okay. Just stay out of it!" Vicky yelled.

"You heard her, homes. Leave her alone."

Vicky turned to see Martin dart between her and Steve. Steve's eyes widened and he stepped back cautiously. He was maybe four inches taller and thirty pounds heavier than Martin. Yet she knew that difference would not stop Martin. She could tell by the hard set to his jaw that he was ready to fight. She couldn't let that happen. Another fight and he would be sent back to Superintendent Gates again. And this time, he wouldn't get a second chance.

"It's fine, Martin," she said quickly, grabbing his shoulder and pulling him back, away from Steve. "We were just talking."

"About what?" Martin demanded. There was an edge to his voice that she hadn't heard before, almost as if he didn't trust her.

"Nothing," she told him firmly. "Steve was just—"

"We were just talking about you, *Sanchez*," Steve cut in. He flashed a smug grin and waited, as if he expected Martin to do something. "What? You don't believe me? Ask her."

Martin glanced back at Vicky. She could tell he wasn't sure what to believe.

"It was nothing, Martin," she said. "Don't listen to him."

"She don't want you to know I'm looking out for her," Steve said.

"That ain't your place, homes," Martin growled. "She don't need you to take care of her."

"C'mon, Martin. Ignore him. Let's go." Vicky pulled at Martin's arm, but it didn't budge.

"No, it *is* my place," Steve snapped. "See, me and her used to be tight. We were friends back when you were just a wannabe thug taggin' walls in the *barrio*. I'm just makin' sure she's okay," he added. "You understand, *homes*?"

Vicky felt Martin's muscles tighten. She knew he was about to snap.

"Boy, you startin' with me again?" he hissed. "Didn't you learn last time?"

"Would you two just quit it! I don't need *anyone* to take care of me," Vicky snapped, tugging on Martin's shoulder. "*C'mon*," she repeated.

Martin shrugged her hand aside. He seemed unable to walk away.

Steve grinned. It was the same mean smile Vicky had seen when Steve shouldered someone on the basketball court or hit someone hard on the football field. Maybe part of him was concerned for her. But another part of him wanted something else—to see Martin go down. Vicky could see it in his eyes.

"Yeah, you should probably go, *Sanchez*," Steve said then. "I know you can't afford to get in trouble again, not after your hearing and all."

Martin's eyes narrowed. Vicky could almost feel the anger burning through his skin like a fever. She knew he was ready to pop.

"*What?* You got somethin' more to

say?" Steve asked mockingly. "What'chu gonna do?"

"Is there a problem here, gentlemen?"

Vicky turned back to see Mr. Mitchell striding down the hallway toward them.

Thank God, she thought to herself.

Martin shook his head and took a deep breath.

"No problem, Mr. Mitchell," Martin said.

"Yeah. Me and Luna just talking, that's all," Steve added. "We cool, right?" As Steve spoke, he stretched out his hand to Martin as if they were friends.

For a second, Martin stared at Steve's raised palm as if it was covered in poison. But as Mr. Mitchell came closer, he reached for it.

"Yeah, we cool, homes," Martin said, grasping Steve's hand and rolling through a tense handshake. Their eyes locked for several seconds. Vicky wanted to yell at them both, but Mr. Mitchell was just a few feet away. If he wasn't, the boys would be fighting again. She was sure of it.

"See, it's just like he told you, Mr. Mitchell. Ain't nothin' to worry about," Steve said, forcing a fake smile. He then dropped Martin's hand as if it was an empty can he had just gulped dry. "Later, Luna!" he added, heading toward the gym.

Vicky nudged Martin toward Bluford's main doors, away from Mr. Mitchell, who eyed them closely as they passed. She could feel him staring at her back as she rushed down the long corridor. She was careful not to go too fast, though she couldn't get out fast enough.

"Man, that dude ain't ever gonna stop," Martin grumbled as they stepped outside.

"Just ignore him. He's just starting with you so you'll do something stupid," Vicky said, looking at her watch. She couldn't stand that she had to go home already, and that all their time together was spent dealing with Steve. The whole afternoon was ruined. "I don't even want to talk about him."

Martin frowned. "Yeah, well, I think he wants to talk about you. I saw the way he was looking at you before I showed up. He's still into you."

Vicky rubbed her temples as her head began to throb. Teresa had said the same thing when she and Steve first broke up.

"*He totally sweats you,*" Teresa had

insisted. *"I see him looking at other girls, but not the way he looks at you."*

Vicky had ignored her, but now she wondered if maybe it was true. She remembered how Steve reacted when she broke up with him. They were at St. Anna's Church carnival last July. Steve had won her a toy tiger by throwing darts at a wall of balloons. After he won, he laughed at a smaller kid next to him who failed to hit anything.

"Man, you should let my girl throw 'em for you," he had joked.

The kid was probably in middle school. He ignored the comment and didn't even raise his eyes to look at them. Steve chuckled when the boy left a few seconds later. He had done similar things before, making Vicky cringe inside. But at that instant, watching the nervous boy walk away, Vicky thought of Danny. She knew how Steve would treat him if he was at Bluford. Danny with his acne, reddish hair, and wiry arms. Steve would target him for sure.

The thought lit a spark inside her, one that spread into a wildfire. An hour later, they were leaving, and she couldn't hold back any longer.

"I can't do this, Steve. I'm sorry, but I

don't wanna see you anymore," she had said finally. She had threatened it before. They were always fighting, but this time was different. Steve seemed to know it.

He was quiet for several seconds. Then he grunted, bit his lip, and lowered his head as if the news was a weight pressing down on his shoulders.

"*I knew this was comin',*" he said, kicking a can across the street. "*You the only one who makes me think about how things were back in the day. And you know what? I'm tired of thinkin', and I'm tired of fighting with you all the time. Do what you gotta do. I ain't stoppin' you,*" he mumbled, keeping his eyes hidden from hers. His voice sounded heavy and hoarse. "*I don't need you anyway. I don't need no one.*"

He had stormed away without looking back. The next day, Vicky heard from Teresa that he had crushed Roylin Bailey in football practice. But for her, it was over. She hadn't seen him all summer, and during the first week of classes, he acted strangely normal, as if they were friends again. But since Martin arrived, everything went sour.

Vicky's mind raced. Her stomach

suddenly felt as if it was sinking.

Maybe Teresa and Martin were right.

Maybe Steve wasn't over her.

Maybe all the trouble with Martin was because of her.

It made too much sense.

"I don't even know why you were talking to him," Martin fumed, breaking her thoughts. "Why did you ever go out with someone like that?"

She could hear the anger in his voice. But there was something else lurking there too that she didn't like.

"It was complicated," Vicky replied. "He wasn't always such a jerk. Besides, I didn't ask him to come to my locker. He came to me," she said, trying to be honest. But as she uttered the words, she could see they bothered Martin.

"What do you mean *complicated?* How come you never told me about this?" he barked. The anger in his voice was sharp and mixed with jealousy. It caught Vicky off guard. Their afternoon was crashing down in jagged pieces all around her.

"What's your problem, Martin?" she shot back, torn between guilt about Martin's troubles and anger at the way he was suddenly hurling questions at her. "Steve and I were never serious."

"Then why do you say it's complicated?" Martin huffed.

Vicky couldn't believe her ears. It was as if Martin felt threatened. "Look, Martin, what do you want me to say? I went out with him for a while, but it's over. You hear me? *Over!* You don't hear me asking you about every girl you went out with."

"Yeah, well that's 'cause I ain't never felt this way before, Vicky. There wasn't anybody else like you, okay? You don't have nothin' to worry about," Martin said. He locked his eyes on hers for a second. They were dark and stormy. She saw the hurt in them. Insecurity. The imprint of painful experiences, events she didn't even know about.

"Martin—"

"C'mon. Let's go to Niko's," he grumbled, walking down the main steps ahead of her, his hands in the pockets of his baggy black hoodie, his shoes scuffing on the steps.

"I can't, Martin," she said.

"What?"

Vicky felt as if she was being pulled in opposite directions, as if she was about to rip in half somehow. "My mom needs me to take care of my grandfather. She left me a message in the office," she explained. "I have to go straight home to be with him."

Martin nodded slowly as the news sank in. She could see he was disappointed.

"Look, I'm sorry. Believe me, I'd rather go out with you than go home," she added. "I can't stand it there right now."

"No problem. You gotta do what you gotta do, right?" he said quickly. Too quickly. Like his words meant the opposite of what he said—that there *was* a problem. He started walking away.

"*Martin—*"

"Nah, it's all good, Vic. I gotta see my counselor tonight anyway, remember? Gonna work on them *anger management* issues," he added. She could hear the bitterness in his voice as he crossed the street.

"Look, I'll call you, okay?" she said.

She thought maybe he mumbled something, but she wasn't sure. A loud truck passed between them, and by the time it pulled away, Martin was halfway down the block, rushing away from her.

He didn't turn back.

Chapter 5

Vicky was almost home when the familiar yellow bus from Irving Middle School lumbered past her and hissed to a stop at the corner of her block. She winced at the loud clap of the doors opening. A second later, Danny stepped out along with a few other kids.

"Yo, pizza face, drop them video games and pick up some soap," yelled a thick-necked boy out of a window near the back of the bus.

"Yeah, he need to wash wit' Brillo or somethin'," another kid chimed in.

"*Brillo!*" someone repeated. "That's cold!"

A roar of laughter erupted behind him. Danny blushed with rage.

"Man, shut up!" he hollered as the bus pulled away in a noisy cloud of smoke.

Vicky hated that other kids teased him. But whenever she tried to talk to him about it, he avoided her or changed the subject. And the last time she stood up for him, Danny had gotten upset and told her to stay out of it. The problem had gotten worse since he started middle school, though Mom and Dad seemed too distracted to notice.

At least he had his friends, she thought, boys like Mario and Javon who lived nearby. Before Dad lost his job, they used to come over after school to play *Doombringer* and *Street Warrior* on the Game Box. Danny was always the best, calling himself *T-Bomb* when he played. He would joke about how he let them win for a short time and then he would explode, like a time bomb, and beat everyone. No matter how hard she tried, Vicky couldn't touch him. His fingers were a blur on the controller. On the screen, he was invincible.

"You should call yourself T-Dork," she would tease, *"'cause sooner or later that's what we're all gonna call you."*

Mario and Javon would laugh along, sneaking glances at her backside when they thought she wasn't looking. Vicky pretended she didn't notice.

"Little sixth grade dogs," Teresa had called them when she witnessed their wandering eyes.

But lately, since Dad was home more, they avoided her house. Instead, they hung out at Mario's apartment with his older brother Felix while their mom was at work. Danny was there most days too. Anything to get away from the stress that filled their house, she figured. Vicky wished she could escape too. Martin's apartment was just a few doors from Mario's.

"What are you looking at?" Danny asked as she approached him on the corner. She realized she had been staring at him.

"Nothing, I'm just thinking, that's all," Vicky said, pretending she hadn't heard what the kid called him or noticed the three painful-looking pimples that dotted his chin. "Mom ask you to come straight home, too?" she asked.

"Yeah," he grumbled, hoisting his navy backpack up on his back.

In the bottom corner she noticed a tiny drawing in black magic marker: a sphere with a lit fuse on top. The fuse was drawn in detail with sparks flying to show it was on fire. Underneath, written in tight block-style letters, was a word. *T-Bomb*.

"Why'd you draw that thing on your backpack?"

"Don't worry about it," Danny replied, adjusting the pack so she couldn't see the picture.

Whatever, she thought. They walked down the street in silence, careful not to make eye contact with the older kids on Union Street or the guys who yelled things out to Vicky as they passed. Within minutes, they were home.

"Abuelo?" Vicky called as she opened the front door to their house. The TV was off. So were all the lights in the living room and kitchen. Danny called out, too. No response.

"Abuelo?" she repeated, raising her voice. She remembered that his hearing was failing. "Abuelo!"

"*Si? Estoy aqui,*" came a faint reply. *I'm here.*

His voice came from the closed door of her bedroom. Vicky sighed with relief. The only thing that could make the day worse was if Abuelo hurt himself, especially while she was supposed to be watching him.

"Are you okay?"

"Okay . . . yes," he answered in English. But his voice didn't match his words. It seemed weaker than usual. Almost pained.

"Can I come in?" Vicky asked.

She heard her grandfather sigh. "I'm okay," he repeated. "I don't need help." Then she heard a dull thud followed by the sound of something sliding on the carpet.

"What's he doing in there?" Danny asked from the edge of the hallway.

Vicky shrugged. *What if he fell again?* she wondered. Last time he slipped, he cracked his hip and lay on the floor for hours, unable to get up. Since then, he had never been the same. Most days, he was sore and stiff and shaky on his feet. Mom said he was too stubborn to admit he needed help. That was why she insisted that he move in with them. Vicky imagined he was on the other side of the door, stretched out on the floor, hurt but unwilling to tell anyone.

I have to make sure he's okay, she thought to herself. Danny seemed to agree. He waited at the door's edge, nodding to her as she turned the doorknob.

Inside, Abuelo was sitting on her bed, his eyes puffy and red. His shoulders slumped when he saw her, as if he had given up whatever he had been trying to hide.

"*Niña,*" he said, gently wiping his eyes. "*Mira.*" *Look.*

Vicky scanned the room and noticed her bed was covered with old photographs, many of them yellowed with age.

"See how beautiful?" he said, carefully picking up a framed black and white photograph he had placed on her nightstand. "Just like you."

Vicky's eyes locked on a woman in a flowing white dress. A delicate veil gracefully draped her curly black hair, framing her face. Her arched eyebrows were just like Mom's. She seemed to gaze from the photo, as if she knew a journey of years lay ahead. Next to her stood a handsome black-eyed man with his hair slicked back. Vicky thought he almost looked like an old-fashioned movie star. His arms gently encircled her. His palms rested lightly on her forearms, as if he was afraid to touch her too strongly.

"Is that who I think it is?" Danny asked.

Abuelo nodded somberly. "That's our wedding picture. Fifty-six years ago, God

66

bless her," he said, pausing for several seconds. In the silence, Vicky could almost see the thoughts racing through his mind.

"*I* was supposed to go first, not her," he added, his eyes glistening, his hands trembling.

"Abuelo—"

"What do I do now?" he asked, looking to each of them and then back at the picture, as if he was talking to it, waiting for an answer that would never come. "What do I do?"

The air grew heavy and silent. Vicky didn't know what to say. She wished her parents were there, that Mom could step in and comfort him somehow. Unsure what to do, Vicky put her arms on his bent shoulders, hugging him. She could feel her grandmother's chain tug at her neck. For several moments, no one said a word.

"Abuelo, is all this yours?" Danny said then, pointing to an open suitcase at the foot of her bed. She could tell her brother was trying to change the subject.

"Yes, I was unpacking. Must keep busy," he said, his voice calming. "*Mira*," he added. He wanted them to look at something.

Vicky turned and noticed more framed pictures, a stack of old envelopes tied with string and two musty shoe boxes. One of them was open. Inside were piles of color photographs she recognized.

A picture of herself graduating from kindergarten. Danny at his first communion. A family shot with all of them at the beach.

"I remember that day," Danny said, pointing to the beach photo. Dad was on his knees in the sand holding each of them on his shoulders, his arms curled like a weightlifter.

"Me too," Vicky said, recalling how Dad's pale back had turned bright pink with sunburn. But it didn't stop him from scooping them in his arms and carrying them into the water. That day Dad had taught them to body surf, something he said he had learned on the beaches of New Jersey, where he used to go as a child.

"I'm scared," Danny had said when Dad first took him in the water.

"Don't be scared, buddy. I won't let anything happen to you," Dad replied.

"I don't want to do it," Vicky had said, but Dad convinced her to try it once,

telling her that if she made it all the way to the beach, he would get her some ice cream. It worked.

Vicky could still remember the rise of the waves as they reached their breaking point, the foamy push as they crashed down, rocketing her forward. Her brother laughed so hard, salt water came out of his nose. Mom had teased Dad that his skin was so white, she needed sunglasses to look at him and that he had turned their kids into little beach bums. They responded by splashing her with water until they were all soaked and sandy. Was it the last time she had heard her parents laugh together?

"What happened?" she thought to herself, studying the photo. It was as if she was staring at something that was gone forever, something she could never reclaim, no matter how much she wanted it back. An ocean of sadness stirred inside her, its invisible waves breaking as she glanced at the photo. She dropped it back in the box, as Danny and Abuelo flipped through more pictures.

She wanted to be alone, to go somewhere and forget about the photo, Abuelo's sadness, the fight with Teresa, her worries about her parents, the problems with Martin and Steve. But there was nowhere to escape. She didn't even have a bedroom.

RING!

Vicky jumped as the phone's ring blasted through the house like a car horn. She glanced over at the clock. It was 3:42 p.m., the usual time for the calls to start coming in. Danny didn't even budge. Lately they almost always ignored the ringing, just as Dad told them to.

RING!

"You answer?" her grandfather asked, gesturing toward his ear.

"The answering machine will get it. It's probably for Mom or Dad anyway," Vicky explained.

RING!

"When he was here earlier, your father did not answer either," Abuelo noted.

"Dad was here?"

RING!

"*Si,*" Abuelo said. "He was here for lunch. We ate, and then he left in a hurry. Moving too fast."

Vicky figured that Dad was looking for work again, maybe rushing to get to an interview or something. The phone finally stopped ringing and Vicky listened as the answering machine picked up. A second later, she heard an electronic voice leaving a message.

"This is an urgent call regarding a past-due account," the voice droned.

Vicky knew the next part of the message. She had heard it all before. It started over the summer when their cell phone company started calling about unpaid bills. Shortly after, all their wireless phones were shut off. Now other companies called. Credit cards. Banks. Collection agencies. Vicky had gotten used to the calls, but she knew Abuelo might worry if he knew bill collectors were calling. She rushed to the kitchen to turn the volume down on the answering machine.

"Immediate action is required in order to prevent—"

Vicky silenced the machine, her face hot with embarrassment. Dad had told them a while ago to ignore the messages, but what about Abuelo? She hoped with his weak hearing and with Danny talking to him, he hadn't heard the message. More than that, she just wished the calls would stop once and for all.

That's not gonna happen, she thought.

Without a word, she escaped to the living room, flopped on the couch, and turned on the TV. The screen filled with a garbled image. The TV hissed with static, as if it was cursing at her.

"Great!" she mumbled, flipping the channels. None of them worked. "I can't believe this."

"What?" her brother said from the bedroom.

"The TV's out," she said.

"You serious?" he said, walking over to the TV and messing with the cables in the back. "Think we should call Mom?"

Vicky shook her head, realizing what the problem was. Next to the answering machine was a stack of bills. Many of them were unopened. Some were from the cable company. She had seen them for weeks. She was sure their service had been cut off because they hadn't paid their bill.

"No. Just wait for Mom or Dad to come home," she said, clicking the TV off.

Silence filled the room, making Vicky feel trapped. It was as if the walls of their home were closing in on them, as if each day the rooms got smaller and smaller. Yet she was powerless to stop it.

A burning acid taste crept into her mouth again, the same one she had felt whenever her parents were fighting.

CLUNK!

Vicky looked up to see Abuelo's shoulder nudge against the door of her room. He grunted with effort to keep his balance, his hands white-knuckled on his walker. He was trying to reach the bathroom.

Instantly, Vicky rushed to his side.

"I don't need help. I'm fine!" he huffed in Spanish, struggling to maneuver the walker into the hall. "I'm a man, not a baby!"

Vicky ignored his words and her own pounding headache as she helped steer him across the hallway. He labored with each step, a sight that made Vicky cringe. Danny watched nearby, shaking his head at what he had seen, as if he was in pain too.

Abuelo closed the door and Danny sighed, heading into the living room. Vicky walked back across the hall to her room, scanning the pictures still on her bed. Her grandmother stared back from her wedding photo, young and frozen in time. Blind to what was happening to her family.

"Maybe it's better that way, Grandma," Vicky said, resting her hand on her neck chain.

In the distance, she heard the sound of electronic gunshots. Danny was playing *Doombringer* again. Behind her, the bathroom pipes creaked. Abuelo was washing his hands. He would need her help again any second.

Vicky closed her eyes and tried to rub away the pain in her temples and relax the queasiness in her stomach. But it wasn't working. She couldn't shake the feeling that her whole world was unraveling right beneath her feet.

Chapter 6

"Don't do this. Please."

Vicky opened her eyes at the sound of her father's voice. It was tense and urgent. She heard his footsteps pace across the kitchen, what he did lately whenever he was on the phone.

"I just need more time," he said just above a whisper.

Vicky turned and looked at the clock. It was just after 8:00 on Saturday morning.

Weak light filtered through the dusty window blinds, making the living room ghostly gray. She realized she had never called Martin. She had hoped to speak with him last night and see how his appointment with the counselor went, but instead she'd opened her English textbook and passed out on the couch.

She could barely recall falling asleep, though she had a dim memory of her parents arguing and Dad pulling a blanket snug around her neck.

Did he say "Sorry Princess" when he did that? The memory was so foggy she wasn't sure.

"Look, I'm doing everything I can," Dad said just above a whisper. "Things I never dreamed I'd do just to try to raise this money. Give me more time. This is our home you're talking about."

There was a pause. Vicky held her breath, unable to stop herself from listening.

"You don't understand," he replied, his voice sounded more frustrated than ever. She pulled the blanket up over her face.

"C'mon, work with me here. *Please!*"

He cursed then, slamming the phone down.

Vicky pretended to be asleep as he stormed into the living room, grabbed something and headed out the front door. He made several trips outside carrying bags and boxes. Then she heard his car start, and he was gone.

Not long after, she heard the click and thump of her grandfather's walker pressing on the carpet.

Not now. It's Saturday. Can't you at least sleep late, Abuelo? she wanted to say.

She peeked from her blanket to see her grandfather coming slowly down the hall. But rather than come into the living room, he turned and headed into the kitchen, grunting with effort.

"Papi, what are you doing?" Mom asked, following him from her bedroom. Her eyes were blotchy and swollen, as if she hadn't slept at all the night before. "Just go sit with Vicky and I'll make breakfast," she said.

"No!" he barked. "I'm tired of sitting."

Her mother shook her head in frustration. She looked exhausted.

"I'll help him, Mom," Vicky said, stretching and getting up from the sofa. Mom retreated zombie-like to her room as Vicky dragged herself to the kitchen. Inside Abuelo had opened the refrigerator and was pulling out ingredients and placing them on the counter.

Eggs. Cheese. Salsa. Butter. Leftover refried beans Mom had made the other day.

"Abuelo, what are you doing?" Vicky asked.

"Making breakfast," he replied, as if her question was silly.

"But Abuelo, you can't even . . ." she began but then stopped herself. She didn't have the heart to say the words to him.

He stopped and turned to her as if he knew what she was about to say.

"One day you'll be old and understand, *niña*," he said then. "I *have* to do something."

Vicky heard the emotion in his voice. It was almost as if he was desperate too, just like Dad.

"Well, then let me help you," she insisted, putting an arm around his shoulders.

He studied her face, his eyes glimmering slightly. "You're so much like your grandmother. Even more than your mother," he said, shaking his head. "Okay, you can help me, *niña*. Get me some flour and two pans."

For the next hour, Vicky followed Abuelo's orders, mixing dough by hand, dividing it into round clumps, letting them sit for a time, and then rolling them carefully on the table. Though his fingers were gnarled and leathery, Vicky noticed they seemed to soften and become flexible when he worked the dough, transforming it into homemade tortillas, something she hadn't eaten in years.

"Not too thin or they break," he explained as she followed his example. With his help, Vicky heated the tortillas, covered them in scrambled eggs, salsa, and refried beans. He even taught her how to make fresh coffee for Mom.

"What smells so good?" Danny said, walking into the kitchen while Vicky was setting the table.

"Abuelo made breakfast."

"For real?" Danny looked astonished.

"Vicky made it, not me," Abuelo said with a playful wink. "Sit down and eat before it gets cold. *Yolanda!*" he called to Vicky's mother as if she was a little girl.

Mom walked in looking as exhausted as ever, though the sight of the table brought a smile to her face. Vicky loved the way Mom's smile brightened the room. It was the first time she had seen it in a while.

"Wow, it smells so good in here," Mom said, giving Abuelo a kiss. "If you two do this every day, I'm gonna have to go on a diet." She then squeezed Vicky's arm warmly. Vicky knew it was her way of saying thank you, and she felt the cloud over the house lift a bit.

For once, the table was full of good food and no one was yelling or fighting. For once, there was no tension lurking in the room like a ghost. And yet, Vicky couldn't avoid staring at the empty seat at the head of the table. Danny seemed to read her thoughts.

"Where's Dad?" he asked.

"He said he's got an early interview this morning. A good dealership in the suburbs. Pray he gets the job," Mom said, sipping her coffee, her eyes gazing toward the front door. "We need all the help we can get."

Abuelo grunted. Vicky knew something wasn't right about Mom's answer. Her father didn't seem as though he was talking about a job interview when she'd heard him in the kitchen. And why was he loading the car if he was going to an interview? It didn't make sense. Yet she didn't want to say anything, especially not with Abuelo listening. Instinctively she reached for her cross.

It was gone.

She ran her hand along her neck and realized that the whole chain was missing. Had it broken? Maybe she had snapped it when she was cooking. She looked in her seat and then back at the kitchen floor. Nothing.

"What is it, Vicky?" said Mom.

"My necklace. It's miss—"

RING!

The kitchen phone blared like an alarm clock. Abuelo dropped his fork.

"*Adios Mio!* It isn't even 10:00 yet!" he exclaimed.

"Why don't they just leave us alone?" Danny groaned. Mom grimaced as if the sound hurt her ears too.

RING!

What if it was Martin? Vicky wondered. She decided to grab it, just in case.

"Hello?"

She heard an electronic click and immediately knew it was another collection agency, transferring the call to a real person. Her pulse quickened.

"Michael Fall-on?" the caller said, mispronouncing her last name.

Vicky could hear other voices in the background. Laughter. Countless other calls being made. Other people being hassled for money. She wondered about the person on the other end of the phone. Did he know what it was like to be harassed at all hours of the day? Did he even care that her father was out of work, her grandfather was ill, and her mother was struggling? It was as if money was the most important thing in the world. Vicky hated it.

"Wrong number," she declared. She then hung up the phone and turned to her mother, unable to stop the question from jumping from her lips.

"Mom, when's this gonna stop? It's getting worse, not better," she said. It was the first time she had ever asked her directly about the phone calls. Danny and Abuelo turned toward Mom. Their expressions said they were also interested in her answer.

"Your father and I are behind on some bills," her mother admitted.

"Why didn't you tell me before you asked me to come here?" Abuelo muttered. "You don't need an old man to take care of right now!"

"No, Papi. I didn't tell you 'cause I didn't want you to worry. Michael and I are fine. I mean, yes, with him out of work, things are a little tight. But they're tight for a lot of people right now. The car payment, insurance, the mortgage, bills, credit cards. I mean we didn't know he'd lose his job," she said, shaking her head. "No one's buying cars right now."

"What's gonna happen?" Danny asked then. He seemed younger and more vulnerable somehow. "We hear the messages. I see the mail. Now the TV's not working. It's like each day, things get worse, and the way you and Dad are acting lately . . ." his voice trailed off.

Vicky's stomach churned at Danny's words. She could hear the worry and pain in them. She reached for her missing chain. Danny stabbed at his refried beans.

"How are we acting?" Mom snapped defensively. "If you were the only one taking care of everything all the time, you'd get upset too," she added, pausing to take a deep breath. She glanced around the table at the many eyes which were suddenly locked on her face.

For a second, the room was completely silent, as if everyone was hanging on her words.

"Look, don't you worry. Your father's at an interview right now. Sooner or later, something is going to break for him. You'll see. Until then, we're just gonna have to sit tight," Mom said. But her voice was hollow, as if she didn't fully believe what she said. She raised the coffee cup to her mouth like she was trying to hide behind it. The sight gave Vicky a chill. Abuelo looked as if his breakfast had upset his stomach.

"Enough about this. These things are for your father and me to worry about, not you. Your job is to keep up with your schoolwork, okay?" Mom said, her voice sounding forced and unnatural. "How are the plans for Teresa's *quinceañera* coming along? Did she pick out her dress?"

Danny rolled his eyes and got up from the table. Abuelo watched him go, so did Mom, though no one said anything. Vicky wanted to get up, too. More than anything, Mom's assurances made her more worried, not less. The last thing she wanted to think about was Teresa's stupid party.

"I have no idea," she answered, watching Danny escape to the living room. "I'm not going."

"Not going? Why not? The two of you are best friends—"

"I'm just not going, okay?" Vicky snapped. She wasn't about to mention the money issue or Teresa's problems with Martin. It was bad enough without

Mom getting involved.

"It's not about your *quinceañera* is it? You know if money wasn't so tight, we'd a had a big—"

"No it's not that, Mom. Just forget it, okay?" Vicky said, feeling a wave of resentment. She got up from the table and took her plate to the sink.

"Where's my Game Box?" Danny yelled from the living room.

"Huh?" Vicky said.

"Did you take it?" he asked accusingly.

"What are you talking about?"

"My Game Box. It was here yesterday, and now it's gone. Someone musta stole it."

"No one stole it," Vicky replied. "How could that happen? Someone's always here. And if someone stole it, I woulda heard it. Remember, I was sleeping on the couch."

As she spoke, Vicky remembered what she had heard earlier, the sounds of her father taking things to his car. A chill raced down her spine as she remembered his conversation.

"*I'm doing things . . . I never dreamed I'd do,*" he had said. Did that include taking things from their house? Is that what Dad meant? The questions tumbled through her mind.

"Maybe Dad took it," she said.

"*Dad?*"

"Why do you say that?" Mom asked, her eyes suddenly stormy.

"I heard him this morning when he left. He took a bunch of stuff to the car."

"I thought you said he was looking for work today," Abuelo said in Spanish.

"That's what he told me." Mom pushed her plate away as she spoke.

"You mean Dad stole my Game Box?!" Danny exclaimed, his voice a mix of hurt and outrage.

"He didn't steal it," Mom said, a little too forcefully. "If he took it, there was a good reason."

"Yeah, right! My games are gone too," Danny blurted, rushing to his room and slamming the door behind him. Abuelo mumbled a prayer in Spanish.

In the distance, Vicky could hear Danny's drawers opening and closing. He emerged a minute later dressed in jeans and a black T-shirt, his backpack hung on his back.

"Where you goin'?" Vicky asked.

"Mario's," he said, racing for the door. His eyes were puffy and pink as if he had been crying.

"For what?" Vicky asked. But he ignored her, dashing out as if the house was on fire.

Chapter 7

Vicky's pulse pounded in her head like a hammer. Waves of queasiness rolled through her stomach. With the TV off and Danny and Dad out, the house felt unnaturally quiet, like the hush of a breath before a scream.

She forced herself to clear the table and wash the breakfast dishes. Abuelo struggled to help her, though neither of them said a word. In her mind, Vicky kept seeing the pained look on Danny's face as he had run out.

"You're worried about him, aren't you?" Abuelo said finally. Mom was in her bedroom vacuuming, something she always did when she was upset.

"Huh?"

"Your brother. I worry too. You should go check on him. He's not as strong as you."

Vicky stopped and stared at her grandfather. "I don't feel strong," she admitted. Her eyes burned for an instant.

"*Niña*, you're carrying too much on your shoulders right now," he said, putting his hand on her back. "I don't know why God makes things happen the way they do. If Carolina was still with us, we would take you and Danny out of this house for a while. But she's gone, and I'm too old to do that now."

"Abuelo—"

"No, listen to me, *niña*," he said, cutting her off. "Yesterday I asked your grandmother why she left me. What am I supposed to do? This morning, watching you and Danny, I realize she give me an answer. I'm here to help you two and your mother. That's going to be my job from now on," he said firmly. His face almost seemed younger somehow. Stronger.

Vicky smiled, grateful he was there with her. Yet looking at him, with his walker and gnarled fingers, she didn't know what he could do about their family's troubles. "Thanks, Abuelo," she said, trying her best to hide her doubts.

"Now go," he said, taking the dish towel from her. In the distance, she heard the whirring roar of the vacuum cleaner. "Your mother and I need to talk."

Vicky showered and put on her favorite jeans and a snug ribbed tank top just in case she would see Martin. Her jeans, which once hugged her hips perfectly, seemed a bit loose. Had she lost weight? Mom's scale said Vicky was six pounds lighter than she had been a few weeks ago. She knew she had been eating less. Most days, especially when her parents were fighting, she didn't have any appetite. Often her stomach didn't feel right, and she had headaches.

Great. Something else to worry about, she thought.

She examined her face. Even her olive skin seemed a little greenish in the gray light that filtered in through the bathroom window. She put on some makeup to hide it and ran her fingers through her long black curls, hoping that once she checked on Danny, she could visit Martin. Maybe they could even steal a few minutes together, anything to patch the awkward moment in school yesterday.

Outside, a weak breeze swirled bits of trash at her feet as she headed toward Mario's apartment. She passed the small park where she and Martin had spent time just two weeks earlier. Three guys were sitting at the bench where they had held hands. The guys were a few years older, maybe in their early twenties. One of them was smoking a cigarette and watching her approach.

Vicky noticed him, but her eyes locked on something else. A low brick wall behind them. It was covered with graffiti just as it had been before. But amidst the messy tags and sloppily sprayed names was something new.

A sphere painted in silver and black with a lit fuse. Beneath it were words that made her stomach sink.

T-Bomb.

It was exactly like the one on Danny's backpack, only it was bigger and newer than almost everything else on the wall. As she looked at it, she remembered seeing something just like it on the outside wall of SuperFoods the day of Martin's hearing. She knew instantly it was Danny's work. Abuelo was right. He *was* in deep trouble.

"Yo girl, whatchu starin' at?" yelled the man with the cigarette, snapping her from her thoughts.

"Yeah, don't you know it's rude to stare?" his friend hollered.

"Hey *mamacita*, why don't cha c'mon over and sit with us instead," the third guy joked, pointing to the empty seat next to him. "I got a spot for you right here." He then mumbled something, and all three of them chuckled crudely.

Vicky ignored them and picked up her pace, rushing several blocks to Hillside Manor, the name of the apartment complex where Mario lived. The community was a cluster of boxy stucco buildings in a U-shape around a courtyard of dead grass. At the front, a small awning marked the rental office. An orange sign in the dirty window announced "Apartments Available."

Vicky ran through the gate toward the back of the complex, racing up the stairs to a second floor unit, number 224. She was out of breath as she pounded on the door. She could see the light in the tiny peephole flicker. Someone was watching her. For several seconds, she heard muffled voices on the other side of the door. Finally, the locks on the door clicked, and the door opened.

Felix, Mario's older brother, stood before her in baggy khakis and a T-shirt. He dropped out of Bluford three years ago and worked at a car wash not far away. A tattoo of a skull with a heart behind it was visible just beneath the sleeve on his bicep. Beneath it was a name: Rosa.

He sipped a can of soda slowly before turning to her.

"Wassup, Vicky?" he said, examining her curiously. "You feeling all right?"

"I'm fine," she said, uncomfortable in his gaze. "Is my brother here?"

"*Danny?*" he said as if the name was unfamiliar to him. Then he paused a bit too long before responding. "Nah, I didn't see him today. Why you lookin' for him?"

Vicky was almost certain he was lying, that Danny was inside listening to her.

"I just need to talk to him, all right? Is Mario home?"

"He's here, but he's still sleeping," Felix said. This time the answer was too quick, like a lie he'd made up just a second ago. He seemed to realize this and took another swig from his soda can. He stood in the doorway so she couldn't see into the suddenly quiet apartment. "Something wrong?"

"Look, I just need to talk with him. If you see him, send him home, okay?" She didn't want Felix to know what was happening at home.

Felix nodded, watching her closely.

"Thanks," Vicky replied. Part of her wanted to barge into the apartment and begin searching it. Instead she walked slowly down the stairs and around to the other side of the complex. She could see Martin's door. The last time she had been to his apartment, he had cried in her arms over his brother, Huero. The memory flooded through her, pulling her across the courtyard like a thirst.

After everything that happened, she wished she could just crawl into his arms, erase all the confusion from school, and bury herself in his chest. Then they could just forget about everything else. It would just be the two of them. No family falling apart. No brother in trouble. No stupid misunderstandings at the end of a school day. Just the two of them alone in his apartment with the world and all its problems locked outside. It was a fantasy she wanted to make real.

Outside his door, Vicky hesitated. What if his mom was home? What would she think about a strange girl at the door looking for her son? Would she think Vicky was trouble? Her hands grew cold and clammy. Her stomach became a quivering knot of nerves. Twice she raised her hand to the door, only to lower it. Finally she couldn't take it anymore. She knocked.

She heard footsteps, and then the door opened to reveal Martin's mom. For a second, her mind went blank.

"Hi, Mrs. Luna . . . I go to school with Martin and—"

"I remember you," Mrs. Luna interrupted, her eyes widening as she spoke. "You were at the hearing the other day. You're Vicky, right? The one who helped Martin."

"Yes—"

"I'm so glad to meet you!" Mrs. Luna beamed, giving her a warm hug. "I never got a chance to thank you for helping him. He's lucky to have a friend like you."

Vicky cringed inside at the word she used. *Friend.* Is that how Martin had described her? After the way he had stormed off on Friday, maybe that was all they were going to be. "Is Martin here?" Vicky asked, struggling to hide her feelings.

"No. He's visiting his brother at the cemetery. It's three months since he died," she said, her voice wavering for a second.

Vicky winced. "I'm sorry," she said, feeling a wave of guilt. She had no idea Martin had such a sad anniversary on his mind this whole week. Why hadn't he told her? And yet, she knew she hadn't told him anything about her troubles either. They had barely talked.

"It's okay," Mrs. Luna said quickly, wiping her eyes. "He goes when he needs to think. He said he'd be back at dinnertime. Why don't you call him then?"

"I will," Vicky said, feeling sorry for making Mrs. Luna so sad.

"And if there is anything we can ever do for you, Vicky, let me know. Maybe you and your family can come over for dinner or something. We still don't know many people in this neighborhood, and it would be nice to meet someone new."

"That would be great," Vicky said, sure it would never happen. Since he had lost his job, Dad didn't want to see anyone, especially their neighbors.

Mrs. Luna gave her another hug as

they said goodbye. "It's been so hard for Martin since we moved here. I know he gets angry sometimes, like the counselor said. But he's a good boy. Thank you for helping him."

Vicky smiled and walked away, wishing Mrs. Luna had stopped talking to her as if she was Martin's big sister. On her way home, Vicky passed the park again and glanced back at the graffiti-covered wall.

Danny's time bomb blazed like a neon sign.

Whoosh!

A thunderous wave hammered against the beach. Vicky watched the wall of water explode into angry white foam and roll back into the boiling sea. Her father was at the water's edge facing her, the ocean behind him. Danny was in front of him. It was the same beach as in Abuelo's picture. The place where they used to laugh. Only now, the ocean was furious. The waves roared and growled hungrily at them.

"C'mon, buddy," Dad said, holding his hand out to Danny. "I won't let anything happen to you."

Vicky could see the ocean building

behind him. A wall of water the color of a deep bruise.

"No, Dad!" Vicky yelled, but her voice wasn't loud enough against the pounding waves. They couldn't hear her.

The wave loomed closer, piling up higher, a moving mountain of water already taller than her father. Danny cried, but her father ignored him, grabbing his little hand and yanking him forward.

"No!" Vicky screamed, rushing toward the water.

Danny and Dad were too close. The wave roared at them like a jet plane. Vicky tried to reach them, but the sand was too thick. It swallowed her feet and held her still.

NO!

An avalanche of water crashed down on Danny and Dad. She watched them vanish in the angry surf. Then she heard her father scream.

"Princess!" Dad called. He held Danny in one arm and flailed helplessly with the other. Danny was motionless. They were being dragged out to sea. "Help!" Dad gasped, choking against the water. He tried to swim, but the current was too strong. His head bobbed under the surface.

Vicky reached the water's edge. She lunged into the froth with all her might, but they were already too far gone.

"Princess . . ." Dad said weakly, his eyes full of sadness as the sea pulled him away. He disappeared beneath the waves. Danny sank with him.

Vicky screamed.

She bolted upright, covered in sweat. Her English notebook tumbled to the floor. She was on the living room couch. Danny sat across from her reading a comic book. She looked at the clock. It was just past 5:00 p.m.

"Bad dream?" Danny said.

"When did you get here?" she replied, ignoring him.

"A little while ago. Abuelo said to let you sleep. He's gonna try to cook tacos for dinner. Mom went to the grocery store to get stuff for him."

"Dad here?"

"Nah," Danny mumbled, flipping the pages in the comic. She could tell he wasn't really looking at anything. "Why'd you come to Mario's today?"

Vicky wiped the sweat from her face and took a deep breath. With their parents gone, she knew she had a chance to talk with him.

"I know what you've been doing, Danny."

"Huh?"

"*T-Bomb*. I can't believe you been taggin' our park! You can go to jail for that, Danny. They've been trying to keep it clean for years, and there you go like some wannabe thug throwing up your little design and messing it up for everyone—"

"It ain't no *little design*. That's *me* up there," Danny huffed. "And it looks good, just like one of these," he said, holding up the comic. "I knew you wouldn't get it. That's the only place, you know, where I feel like I'm doin' something real. School, this house, this place—it ain't real, and you know it."

Just then she heard the thud of a car door outside. Danny went to the window. "Great. Dad's here. You're gonna tell him, right? So what. He ain't even gonna do nothin'. He don't even care anymore," Danny added bitterly.

"That's not true, Danny, and you know it."

Just then, Dad stormed into the front door, his face even more flushed than usual. His jaw clamped down as if he was in pain. He smelled of smoke and alcohol. He moved as if the world was invisibly chained to his shoulders. He looked beaten and broken somehow. It gave Vicky a chill.

RING! The phone screamed to life. Vicky winced. *Not now*, she thought.

In the kitchen, Vicky heard the familiar metallic snap of Abuelo's walker. A second later, she heard his scratchy voice with its heavy Mexican accent.

"Hello? Who? Hold on. Michael," he said, holding out the phone. "For you."

Her father rubbed his temples as if he was in agony. As if he was a balloon about to pop. "Why did you answer the phone?" Dad growled. "This is still *my* house, Diego. Next time, don't answer the phone."

"I'm just tryin' to help, Michael," Abuelo said.

"*Help?!*" Dad scoffed. His face twisted into a bitter scowl as he moved toward the kitchen. "You can't help us. You can't even help yourself."

"Leave him alone, Dad. He didn't do nothing wrong," Danny spoke up.

"You stay out of this!" Dad hollered, walking toward the phone. His face was red with anger. "You want to help, Diego? Here's how you can help."

Vicky watched in horror as her father

yanked the phone from Abuelo's hand, knocking him off balance. Abuelo grabbed the counter to keep from falling but still lost his balance and sank to the floor with a yelp.

"Dad, what are you doing? You could hurt him!" Vicky yelled.

Danny stepped in Dad's path, but her father shouldered him aside, sending Danny slamming against the wall with an ugly thud.

Vicky couldn't believe her eyes. Her father had been transformed. It was as if some horrible beast inside him had suddenly been set free. A bomb long-ticking had finally exploded. She knew she had to act.

Dad whirled around and grabbed the base of the phone and yanked.

Crack! He ripped it free, leaving a gaping hole in the wall.

"Now we'll finally have some peace!" he fumed, his face purple with rage. He held the base in his hand like an upraised hammer. He loomed over Danny, his eyes wild with fury.

Danny raised his arms to protect his head. Vicky was sure Dad would strike him.

"No!" she yelled, darting between her

brother and father, covering Danny as best she could. She braced herself for pain she knew was coming. "Stop, Dad!" she screamed. "Stop!"

Her father let out a wild, angry grunt and hurled the phone into the opposite wall.

Wham!

It exploded against the cabinet in a shower of metal and plastic shards. For an instant, the room was deathly still.

Vicky gazed up at the man in front of her. He had her father's face. The same height and weight, the same close-cropped Caesar cut and goatee. He wore the same dark pants and pressed shirt she had seen him wear since she was a little girl.

But this man wasn't her father. Her father had never tossed her brother aside as if he was a rag doll or sent Abuelo sprawling to the ground. Her father had never screamed at them in blind rage. Most of all, no matter how angry he had been, her father had never made her as scared as she was right now.

A line had been crossed.

Her father huffed as if he had just run a race. His hands clenched and unclenched at his sides. He almost seemed unaware of them, as though he was struggling with something only he could see. Then, with a deep sigh, he rubbed his eyes and winced as if he was in great pain.

"Are you hurt?" Dad said, his voice trembling. Abuelo shook his head as Vicky gently helped him up. Danny turned away, tears glistening in his eyes. While his body seemed okay, Vicky could see something inside Danny had been broken.

"Vicky . . . Danny . . ." Dad said then in a voice filled with sorrow and regret, a sound that tore at her insides like a dull knife. "I-I'm so sorry." He stretched his arms open as though asking for a hug. "It's just . . . these bills, this house . . . I lost it all . . ." He shook his head wearily and Vicky saw tears in his eyes. "I'm sorry."

Vicky wanted to move but couldn't. She wanted to tell him that it was okay, that she understood and forgave him. She wanted to be able to hug him and go back to how things used to be, but she couldn't budge. All she could do was see what he had done a moment ago and wonder what might have happened if she hadn't stood in his way.

"Oh Princess, don't look at me that way," her father said then, turning away as if her stare burned him somehow. He left the kitchen and stopped at the edge of the front door. "No matter what happens, remember I love you. I'm so sorry," he said in a pained, choked voice. Then he turned and left the house.

Seconds later, she heard the harsh screech of tires on asphalt.

He was gone.

Chapter 8

"Clear your desks. It's time for a *Hamlet* pop quiz," Mr. Mitchell announced with a playful grin.

The class groaned.

Vicky's head pounded. She and Mom spent most of Sunday discussing exactly what happened when her father stormed out of the house, reliving each detail. When she finally closed her eyes, she could still see Dad's enraged face as he stood over Danny. And she still heard his haunting words.

"*I lost it all . . . no matter what happens . . . I love you.*"

What did he mean? Almost two days had passed, and Dad still hadn't come home. Mom had tried to be strong, saying everything would settle down once Dad had a chance to cool off. But Vicky knew Mom wasn't being fully honest. She heard her crying softly as she spoke about everything to Abuelo Sunday night.

"*¿Dónde está é, Papi? Por qué está haciendo esto?*" she kept asking. *Where is he, Dad? Why is he doing this?*

Since Dad's outburst, Danny had barely said a word. He spent all of Sunday at Mario's, coming home after dinner and burying his face in comic books, as if they were an escape somehow. Vicky didn't have the heart to tell Mom about the graffiti at the park, not with everything else going on.

"C'mon, Mr. Mitchell. Why you gotta start Monday with a quiz?" Roylin protested.

"Relax, Mr. Bailey. As long as you did your homework, you don't have anything to worry about. This one's easy."

Vicky had completely forgotten about her schoolwork. She could barely remember *Hamlet* or anything else right now. A haze filled her mind. She felt as if she didn't belong in class with other kids. She didn't feel anything like them anymore. She knew Teresa was watching her, but she didn't care. What did it matter after she spent the night hearing

Mom cry, after watching Dad practically beat up Danny, after a weekend of wondering if Dad was ever going to come home?

It was as if she was being pulled out to sea, and no one seemed to notice.

Even Martin seemed like a stranger. She had hoped to at least talk to him before the bell, but he didn't give her a chance.

"How come you never called me?" he'd asked at the beginning of class. "Not Friday like you said. Not Saturday. Not yesterday."

"I came to see you."

"Yeah, but then you disappeared. And you don't even answer my calls. What's up with you? You out with someone this weekend or something?" he said, half-joking.

"Just forget it," she said, rushing to her desk as the bell rang.

"Girl, what's your problem?"

Vicky ignored him, blinking back tears of anger and hurt as she sat at her desk. She wanted to explain to Martin that her father had destroyed the one phone in their house, that Martin was the only one she wanted to be close to right now, but he didn't get it. Instead, he was jumping to conclusions again. Why was he making things even more difficult and complicated than they already were? It was as if he didn't trust her.

And how could she explain it all to him now? She was afraid she would lose it if she tried, that she would fall apart and cry right there in the middle of the classroom. She couldn't do that now. Not at school. Not with Mr. Mitchell dropping a quiz on her desk. It was easier to stay quiet, even if Martin was upset.

Vicky scratched her name on the quiz and scanned the list of questions. She didn't know the answers to any of them, not even the first one.

What happens to Ophelia at the end of Act IV?

She looked around the classroom. Everyone was focused on the quiz. She could hear the dull scrape of pens on paper. Normally, she would speed through and be among the first done while others struggled to keep up. But now she was lost.

Vicky flipped the sheet over so she didn't have to look at the blank items anymore. She wished she could just walk out of the classroom. But where would she go? Home? That almost seemed worse.

"Pass up your papers," Mr. Mitchell instructed and then announced that he would go over the answers in class. He circled toward Vicky.

Please don't call on me, she thought as he got closer. *Not now.*

Vicky's head started to sweat. The familiar queasiness gripped her stomach. She had barely eaten breakfast again.

"So Vicky," Mr. Mitchell said. "I saw that you were done early, as usual. Can you tell us the answer to the first question? What happens to Ophelia at the end of Act IV?"

The classroom grew silent. At first, no one even bothered to look at her, as if everyone expected she would answer the question correctly.

But this time was different. Seconds ticked by. People began to turn toward her, first Martin and then Teresa and Steve. They seemed surprised. Vicky wished they would all just turn away. She tried to think of something to say so Mr. Mitchell would skip her.

I can't deal with my homework right

now, Mr. Mitchell! My family's coming apart, and I haven't eaten or slept right in weeks. I'm scared for my brother, and my stomach feels like someone shoved a knife in it. Just leave me alone!

She imagined herself shouting the words, exploding like a bomb in the middle of the classroom. But instead the words caught in her throat. She stared straight ahead, feeling the sweat bead on her forehead.

"Ms. Fallon?" Mr. Mitchell said. She could hear the surprise in his voice.

"*I* know what happens, Mr. Mitchell," Teresa said then. Vicky couldn't tell if she was trying to show off or help.

"Me too," Steve chimed in.

"Thank you," said Mr. Mitchell. "But the question was for Vicky."

"I don't know," she admitted finally, feeling her face burn. "I . . . didn't get a chance to finish."

Vicky heard several students whisper. Someone in the back of the room snickered. Roylin leaned forward at his desk, and his textbook fell to the ground with a loud slap. She wished she could sink through the floor somehow, away from the wide-eyed, opened-mouthed stares. She knew some students thought

111

it was funny that she didn't know the answer. But Martin, Teresa, and Steve gazed at her as if they were watching something they had never expected to see. Vicky focused her eyes on her notebook to avoid their stares. She could still see the hearts she had drawn last week. It seemed like years ago.

Mr. Mitchell spotted them too, sighing as he passed her desk. "See me after class," he said quickly before turning his back to her. "Teresa, can *you* tell us what happened to Ophelia?" he asked.

"She dies," Teresa said, looking over at Vicky.

"How?"

"She, like, loses it over all this drama with her boyfriend and family, and then she falls into the water and drowns."

Vicky tried to block out the words and the stares that still lingered on her.

"That's right. Good, Teresa," Mr. Mitchell said moving to the front of the room and marking something in his grade book. "But some argue that she might have killed herself. Anyone agree with this? If you can find proof in the text, I'll give you extra credit on your quiz."

Several students scrambled to find

proof for their argument. Vicky zoned out, barely following along as the argument went back and forth with Mr. Mitchell prodding them on. She still couldn't believe what had happened. That Dad nearly smashed her brother's skull with a phone. That he had been gone for two days.

"I would never kill myself over some boy. I don't care who he is," Teresa said at one point.

"That's 'cause you never met the right one," Steve replied, patting himself on the chest.

"*Please*," Teresa scoffed.

Vicky wanted to yell at them both for just sitting there joking while her own family was coming apart and her parents wrestled under a mountain of bills. For the first time ever, school seemed completely pointless.

Vicky could feel Martin staring at her. She knew he had once felt the same way. She remembered it from the day they had met. Part of her wished she could just reach out to him, force everyone else out, and lock the classroom door behind them. But another part of her was angry at him for not trusting her, for making things so difficult.

"Good debate," Mr. Mitchell said at the end of class. "Some of you may not like Shakespeare, but look at what he's writing about in this play. Broken families. Anger and resentment. Revenge and betrayal. People scheming against each other. Murder plots. This stuff was written over four hundred years ago. We still wrestle with the same issues today, right? I hate to say it, but maybe Shakespeare's the original gangsta!" he said as the bell rang.

Groans erupted at Mr. Mitchell's comment.

"Yo, that's corny!" Roylin protested.

Steve shook his head as if he couldn't believe what he had just heard.

Vicky wished she could just leave with the rest of the students who rushed out of the classroom. She knew Mr. Mitchell was going to lecture her about her homework, and she had no idea what she was going to tell him. She braced herself, only to see Teresa hovering over her desk. Unlike the last time they talked, she looked concerned, not angry.

"Hey, girl," she began at last, her voice a bit unsteady. "Are you okay?"

Just then, Martin leaned over Vicky's

desk. Instantly, Teresa's expression changed. She rolled her eyes and turned away. "Never mind," she muttered.

Martin eyed her soberly, and Vicky wasn't sure whether he was about to start questioning her again. But before he even spoke, Mr. Mitchell appeared behind him.

"Excuse me, Martin. But I need to talk to Vicky," he said quietly. "Why don't you catch up with her after school?"

Anger flashed on Martin's face. Vicky knew Mr. Mitchell saw it, but she didn't care. She wanted to get out of the classroom, out of Bluford, and away from everyone.

"Please, Martin," he said gently.

"Whatever you say," Martin grumbled, rapping his fist on her desk in frustration as he walked out.

Mr. Mitchell closed the door and turned to Vicky, his expression serious. He paused for a moment, as if he was gathering his thoughts. Vicky felt her anxiety growing with every second.

"I'm sorry, Mr. Mitchell," Vicky said when she could no longer stand it. "I didn't get a lot of sleep last night, and . . ." she hesitated, wondering if she could actually tell him the truth.

"Vicky, you're one of my best students. But I've watched your work in class the past week, and I have to say I'm concerned about what I see," he explained, his forehead creasing as if he was struggling to find the right words.

"I know Mr. Mitchell. I promise it won't happen again—"

"Listen, Vicky. I know this might be difficult to hear, but as your teacher, I feel I need to say it to you. I am worried about your relationship with Martin. Since you two met, you haven't been the same. Do your parents even know about him?"

Vicky's cheeks flamed at the mention of Martin and her parents. She felt as if she was suddenly under a microscope. Never had any teacher asked about her personal life. Never had she given them reason to. But how could she respond?

No, they don't know about Martin, but that's because we don't talk anymore, Mr. Mitchell. All they do is yell and fight. How can I tell them anything? she wanted to say. But instead, she just shrugged, feeling awkward and embarrassed under his gaze.

"Look, what you did to help Martin

116

the other day was great. But I'm not sure your . . . friendship is helping you. Make sure you don't get in over your head with him, okay? You're a good student. Keep it up, and colleges will be happy to accept you in a few years. I don't want to see you mess that up. I've watched too many talented girls in this school run into trouble with boys. Some get serious with a boyfriend and stop paying attention to their grades. Others have gotten pregnant and had to drop out . . ."

Vicky heard Mr. Mitchell's voice continuing, but her mind snagged on one word that made her cringe.

Pregnant.

What did he think she was? She knew he was trying to help, but he was wrong. She and Martin were nothing like he was saying. Not even close. If he misread her relationship with Martin, how could he help her with the problems at home? There was no point talking to him. No one understood what really was happening. Not her friends. Not her parents. Not her teachers.

"That's not a path you want, Vicky. So just slow down, and focus on your work, okay?" he said, as if his words were supposed to be helpful.

"Thanks, Mr. Mitchell," she grumbled, gathering her books without even looking at him. "I'll read the rest of *Hamlet* tonight. Now can I go?"

Mr. Mitchell's forehead creased, like he had just realized that he'd added up all the numbers and reached the wrong answer. "Is there something else going on, Vicky? I've never seen you like this."

"Like what?" she asked bitterly. "No, everything's fine. Just slow down, right?" Vicky repeated, struggling to keep her voice calm. "I need to leave. I don't want to get a detention for being late."

"I can write you a pass—"

"No thanks. I can make it," Vicky said quickly and dashed out of the classroom, leaving Mr. Mitchell standing near his desk, staring at her in confusion.

Chapter 9

Vicky sat dazed through lunch, barely touching her tuna sandwich. She blinked back tears in geometry class. She knew she had been rude to Mr. Mitchell. He'd only been trying to help, but she couldn't stop herself. He had made her feel worse about everything.

It was as if everyone was so used to Vicky the good student, Vicky the big sister, Vicky the helpful friend, that they couldn't understand that she was coming apart inside. It was like she was invisible somehow, hidden in plain sight.

By gym class, Vicky was exhausted. She slumped down on the bench in front of her locker. Her head throbbed worse than ever. She felt weak and light-headed from not eating. Her empty stomach rolled with queasy waves.

Has Dad come home yet? she wondered. *Is he okay?*

Around her, girls laughed and joked as they changed into their gym clothes. Normally, she would join them, but today Vicky couldn't move. Her legs felt like dead weights. Her feet felt glued to the floor. The last thing she wanted to do was play basketball.

"Shouldn't you be getting dressed, Ms. Fallon?" said Ms. Kinney, her gym teacher, standing at the edge of her row of lockers. She paused and eyed Vicky closely. "You don't look so good. You feeling okay?"

My parents are fighting. My Dad left us two days ago. We don't know where he is.

Just thinking about it made her stomach cramp. She wished she could find the words to unburden herself to someone. Instead, she just shook her head and mumbled. "I don't feel very well. It's my stomach. Can I go to the nurse?"

Ms. Kinney felt Vicky's forehead and then studied her face. "Maybe you'd better," she said, handing her a hall pass. A few minutes later, Vicky was standing in the nurse's office.

"What's the matter, honey?" said Nurse Wilkins, a heavyset woman wearing colorful purple glasses.

"My stomach," Vicky admitted, rubbing the spot under her chest. "Right here."

Nurse Wilkins pressed a gentle hand around Vicky's abdomen. "That hurt?"

Vicky shook her head. "Inside. It sort of burns."

"How long has this been going on?"

"A week or so," Vicky told her, trying to remember the first time she had noticed the feeling. It was while her parents were arguing last week. But really, as she thought about it, she realized it was much longer. Several times over the summer, when the tensions at home seemed about to boil over, Vicky had felt a tight, burning feeling in her stomach. It had been months.

"You worried about something? Does it hurt more when there's something on your mind?"

Vicky hesitated. The nurse seemed nice, but she wasn't about to tell her the whole story. "Yeah, I guess so," she said vaguely.

"Have you eaten anything today?"

Vicky shook her head.

Nurse Wilkins frowned. "Mmm, that's a bad combination, child," she muttered. "You think you could eat a little something now? There's some applesauce in that fridge there," she nodded toward a small white appliance. "And I can get you something from the cafeteria if you want it."

The mention of food brought on a wave of nausea. Vicky shook her head.

"No, thanks," she murmured. "If it's okay, I just want to lie down for a little while."

The woman studied Vicky's face. She seemed about to say something but instead nodded. "All right. Go on and lie down. I'll check you at the bell."

Vicky lay back on a blue vinyl cot, and Nurse Wilkins pulled a curtain around her for privacy. She listened as other students wandered in. A freshman named Lionel. A junior named Brisana.

In the dark, Vicky's mind churned over the events of the past few days. *Maybe Dad is home already*, she told herself. *Maybe he got that job. Maybe he and Mom are talking right now. Hugging each other like old times.*

Please let it be true.

"Feel any better?" Nurse Wilkins asked when the final bell rang.

"Maybe a little," Vicky mumbled.

Nurse Wilkins felt her forehead again and helped her off the cot. "Well, sounds to me like you have too much on your plate, Vicky. And sometimes, that can make your stomach hurt. Sometimes it can do serious damage, too," she added. "Now I want you to make sure you get some food in your system so you don't get weak. And if you ask me, I think you might be stressed about something. Talk to someone. Your parents. Some close friends. Someone you can trust. Better to get that stuff out so it doesn't eat you up inside, you hear?"

Vicky nodded. *But what if they're all part of the problem?* Vicky wanted to say.

"And if that pain in your stomach doesn't go away, you need to see a doctor." She pulled a bright blue sheet of paper from the top of a pile. "These places can help if money's tight."

Vicky looked down as Nurse Wilkins handed her a list of free clinics. She almost refused it, just to hide that her family didn't have money to pay. But then she stopped herself, slipping the paper into her pocket.

"I have to go," she said quickly, eager to escape the nurse's stare. "Thank you."

Vicky rushed to her locker. She wanted to get home fast to find out about Dad and check on Abuelo. But as she turned the corner, she found Teresa leaning against her locker, waiting for her.

"All right, enough. What's going on? What's wrong?" she barked. "I heard you went to the nurse's office in gym. Shanetta Greene said you were sick and might be pregnant."

"I'm not pregnant!" Vicky fumed, her head pounding. "I'm just tired."

"Tired?" Teresa scoffed. "I've seen you 'tired.' You're more than tired. You look *busted*," she peered into Vicky's face, frowning. "You got these dark circles under your eyes, and your skin don't look right."

"Thanks a lot. Look, I gotta go," Vicky said, trying to pass by her, but Teresa moved in her way.

"No, wait, Vicky. Seriously, I'm worried, girl. You been acting like a zombie in class. What is it? Are you okay?"

Vicky looked up at her old friend. The

anger and judgment that had been in her eyes lately was gone, replaced by a look of concern. It was as if the bitter words between them had never happened, that Teresa knew something was seriously wrong. Vicky didn't know where to begin.

"Please, Teresa. Just let me go home," she said, unable to look into her face.

"Why won't you talk to me? Before Martin came along, we used to be like sisters, remember?" Teresa said, grabbing her arm. "Did he hurt you?"

Vicky closed her eyes. She could feel them burning. "No, it's not like that," Vicky said, unable to hold back anymore. "It's my family . . ." she choked, struggling to say the words aloud. "They're broke. All they do is fight anymore. The other night, my Dad almost . . . hurt my brother. Dad left home two days ago. He's never done that before. It feels like everything's coming apart, you know?" As she spoke, a dam of emotion broke inside her, and tears ran down her face.

Teresa slipped her arms around Vicky and hugged her hard. "Oh, girl," she murmured. "I'm so sorry. I didn't know. And I thought you and Martin

125

were having problems."

"We are, but that's another story. He doesn't even know about this. No one does," Vicky admitted, telling her quickly about everything that happened in the last few days. "I don't know what's gonna happen. I keep telling myself they'll be okay, but what if I'm wrong? I'm almost scared to go home. I don't know what I'm gonna find there."

"So take me with you," said a voice behind them. Teresa and Vicky turned to see Steve. How long had he been listening? In the distance behind him was Martin, darting through the crowded hallway toward them.

"No!" Vicky groaned, fearing another clash between them. "Look there's nothing anyone can do for me, okay?" she said, wiping her eyes and stepping away from her locker. "I gotta go. My mom and my grandfather are waiting for me."

"Vicky, what's going on? Why are you crying?" Martin asked, his eyes wide with concern and worry. Part of her wanted to tell him, to dive into his arms and forget everything. But there was no time. Abuelo needed her. She couldn't get into everything in the middle of the hallway, not with her grandfather waiting for her, not with Dad missing, not with her brother in trouble. She needed to get home and find out what was happening first.

"I can't, Martin," she said, touching his shoulder. "I'm sorry, but I need to go home right now."

Martin acted as if her touch burned him. "Oh I get it. You can tell *him*, but you can't tell me," he grumbled, looking at Steve.

"It's not like that. It's just that—"

"No, that's *exactly* how it is," Martin protested. "You won't even give me a chance anymore. I can't keep doing this, Vicky. It's not fair."

"Yo, she don't owe you nothin', Sanchez," Steve cut in, glaring at Martin.

"Are you steppin' to me, homes?" Martin growled, his face twisting into an angry sneer.

Vicky couldn't believe what was happening. Everything was spinning out of control again. She couldn't deal with it. She was about to scream when Teresa stormed right by her.

"Can't you two just stop it?" Teresa yelled, pushing in front of both of them so Vicky could pass. They turned toward her as if they were surprised at the strength of her voice. "If you were her friends, you'd listen to her and leave her alone. Right now, you're only making her problems worse. Go home, girl," she added. "I got this."

Vicky glanced back and saw the anger and hurt on Martin's face. She knew she had to talk to him. But not now. Not yet. She had to get home first.

Vicky noticed the dented cardboard box on her stoop as she neared her house. Everything else on her street looked the same. Oil-stained asphalt streets. Cracked sidewalks framing small burned-out lawns. Stucco one-story houses with barred windows.

But the box was unusual. It couldn't have been there long, or else it would have been stolen. Vicky grabbed it and headed inside.

"What is that?" Abuelo asked, as she placed it on the table.

With her grandfather at her side, she peeled back the cardboard and saw a single yellow sheet of paper covered with Dad's messy handwriting. She couldn't help herself. Her eyes scanned the page.

My Dearest Family,

I have lied to you for too long. And I can't bear to tell you the truth in person. You'd be right to call me a coward. Or something worse.

A man is supposed to work. I'm supposed to pay the bills and keep a roof over our heads. When the dealership closed, I couldn't do that. The money stopped coming in, but the bills never stopped. Car payments, insurance, credit cards, the mortgage. You heard the calls.

A while back, I started betting on sports to make some cash. But that only dug the hole deeper. I kept telling myself that I'd find work and my luck would turn. It never happened. We're thousands of dollars in debt. The bank is taking our house. I tried to fight them. I did terrible things, stealing from you so I could raise money. I bet it all and lost.

When I snapped in the kitchen, I crossed a line. Another second, and God knows what could have happened. I would never forgive myself if I hurt you. When I looked in your eyes, I knew it was over. For your mother and me, this has been a long

*time coming. I am sorry we didn't
prepare you.*

*I know you'll land on your feet. I
promise to find you some day when
my luck has changed.*

*Princess, help your mother and
keep up with your schoolwork. Danny,
forgive me. I never meant to hurt
you. I love you both. You are good
kids. I know you'll be okay. Yolanda,
I'm sorry. But you know it's better
this way.*

Love always,
Dad

"No!" Vicky screamed. The room
spun around her. The floor seemed to
rise and sink as if it was being smashed
by violent waves. She slumped down in
a chair, reading the words again in disbelief.

"What does it say?" Abuelo asked.
"What does it say?"

Vicky sank to her knees. Tears
dripped from her eyes, spilling into the
bottom of the box, landing on an old silver necklace. Beneath it was a stack
of papers bound in rubber bands.
Vicky saw the words "Final Notice of
Foreclosure" on one of them. She felt as

if she was going to throw up.

"Look! That's your grandmother's cross," Abuelo said. "How did it get there?"

Vicky closed her eyes. She knew the answer. Dad had taken it but didn't sell it. Instead he brought it back. His final act.

"*No!*" she screamed.

Chapter 10

"I hate him. I *hate* him!" Danny yelled, spit flying from his mouth.

He crumpled Dad's note and stormed to his bedroom before racing off to Mario's. "I told you he don't care about us!"

Vicky was too devastated to stop him. She sat on the couch holding her grandmother's cross, trying not to cry.

When Mom came home, she glared at the letter in silence for several minutes, her eyes glistening.

"How could he just walk out on us? How could he just leave us like this?" she asked over and over again. Her sad voice was like a knife in Vicky's chest. She wished she could just hold her ears and block out the sound.

Abuelo tried to comfort them, rubbing Mom's back and telling them everything was going to be okay. But Vicky couldn't see how. Everything was coming apart. And Dad's words haunted her.

"I lost it all. They're taking our house."

What did that mean?

Danny came back a few hours later and went straight to his room, slamming the door behind him. At dinner, Vicky knocked, but he refused to open it.

"Leave me alone," he said. "I don't want to talk to anyone." She could hear an occasional thud as something knocked against the wall.

"What about dinner?" asked Vicky. She turned the knob, and it was locked.

"I ate already. Just go away."

"Why are you being this way? It's me," Vicky pleaded.

"I don't care!"

Mom joined her in the hallway. "Danny, open this door. Now!" she yelled.

"What are you gonna do if I don't?" Danny challenged. "You can't do nothin'."

"Don't talk that way to your mother!" Abuelo yelled then, his scratchy voice suddenly deep. "Now open this door before we break it down."

The hallway was silent. Vicky knew her brother was surprised at Abuelo's response. So was she. After several seconds, the knob clicked. Danny opened the door. His eyes were swollen and wet. A bruise-colored smudge covered one cheek. He looked sad and alone, like a child, Vicky thought. He turned and walked away.

"You okay, Danny?" Abuelo asked, moving his walker closer. Mom rushed in, and Vicky followed her.

The windows were open, but the room stank of paint. On the floor were torn photos of Dad, including the one Abuelo had just given him, when he and Dad were at the beach together. On the wall above Danny's bed was a freshly painted image of a time bomb. Its fuse was lit. Drops of extra paint spilled like tears down the wall. Vicky's jaw dropped.

"Danny!" Mom gasped.

Danny slumped on his bed.

"Why did he leave us, Mom?" he said as tears rolled down his cheeks. "Why did he go?"

Vicky felt her own eyes grow misty. She sat down on the bed next to her brother. For the first time in what seemed like ages, Mom hugged them both.

"We'll get through this," she said.

"Somehow, we'll get through it."

It was past midnight when Vicky finally collapsed on the sofa. It seemed as if she had just fallen asleep when she felt someone tug her arm.

"C'mon, get up, Vicky. I need you today." It was Mom.

Outside a dim, ghostly light bled through the window.

"What time is it?" Vicky asked.

"It's early," Mom explained. "But I'm calling out sick and going to the bank first thing to try and sort out this mess. I need you to stay home with Abuelo in case someone from the bank comes to the house. I'll get the school to send your homework. Make sure Danny gets to school on time. I don't want him missing school, too," Mom ordered, her voice tense.

Vicky nodded, sliding off the sofa and turning on the light. Mom's bloodshot eyes looked like two cracked windows. Vicky knew she hadn't slept at all. Yet there was something new in her face: a grim determination. It was as if she wouldn't let herself be hurt, not while her family needed her, not while Dad's mess threatened them.

"What's going to happen, Mom?" Vicky asked. "Are we gonna lose our house?" Vicky couldn't hold back the questions that had been haunting her since she read Dad's letter.

"I don't know," she said, rubbing her temples. "Your father always took care of this. I never paid any attention to it," she admitted. A spark of anger flashed on her face. "But I have a friend at the bank. Maybe she can help us. That's why I have to go."

Vicky nodded as Mom walked down the dark hallway.

The knock came just after lunch.

Vicky looked out the door and saw a police car. Next to it was a silver truck. Three men stood just behind the officer at the front door.

Vicky opened it nervously. She heard Abuelo moving his walker behind her.

"Is Michael Fallon home?" the officer said.

Vicky paused. "He's not here," she replied, eyeing the men. "I don't know when he'll be back."

"Are there any adults here?"

"Yes, my grandfather," Vicky said. "But he doesn't speak English so well. My mother will be back soon," she added.

The officer took a deep breath as if what he had to say was difficult. He then looked past Vicky toward her grandfather.

"Sir, we're here under an order from the court. This home was issued an eviction notice over two weeks ago. You had until yesterday to move out."

"Huh? What are you saying?" Vicky asked. "We never got any notice!"

"You did, Miss. It was signed for by Michael Fallon. I'm sorry, but your family must be out of this house by the end of the day today. All your belongings must be moved out, too."

"You can't do that! Where are we gonna go?"

"I'm sorry, but I must ask you to step out of the way."

"This is my daughter's home. What are you doing?" Abuelo asked in broken English.

"I'm sorry, sir, but a judge ordered this decision," the officer explained. "There's nothing we can do." He then turned to the men. "Do what you need to do."

"Wait!" Vicky protested. But the men ignored her, stepping into the living room. None of them even looked at her. It was as if they didn't want to see her face.

Dad! Where are you? Vicky thought to herself. She looked outside in the hopes that he would pull up, chase the men out, and tell them it was all a big misunderstanding. But he wasn't there. Only a gray truck and the police car were outside.

Dad, please!

A second later, one of the men walked by carrying the nightstand from her parents' bedroom. Two other men grabbed the kitchen table and moved it outside. The officer watched as they worked.

"I think you're all making a mistake. My mother went to the bank today to try to straighten this out. Can't you just come back later, after—"

"Excuse me, miss," interrupted one of the workmen. He was carrying one of their kitchen chairs. He looked uncomfortable, as if he wished he didn't have to be there either.

"All I know is my office received orders from the court to remove your family from the premises by 5:00 p.m. today," the officer said with a sigh. He stepped aside to allow two moving men to carry Danny's bed frame out of the house.

"I'm sorry, I really am," he added. "But this house now belongs to Pacific View Bank. Your family is being evicted."

"No!"

Vicky felt as though someone had kicked her in the face. Her eyes blurred with anger. She could barely see and hardly breathe. The whole world seemed to spin for a long dizzying second.

"No!" Abuelo's voice brought her back to herself. "Vicky!"

He was standing at the edge of her bedroom as if he was guarding it. He gestured for her to come to him.

"I'm sorry, Abuelo. I don't know what to do. We have no phone. I can't even call Mom."

"Listen, *niña*. I have money," he said in Spanish. "I can help. Your grandmother and me. We saved for you and Danny."

"Excuse me, but I'm gonna have to ask for you to move. This room must be cleared," insisted the officer.

The two workmen stepped around them, grabbed her mattress and hoisted it out. Underneath were the suitcases that her grandfather had brought last week.

"These things are mine," Abuelo said, waving his hand. "Don't take them."

"Sir, everything must go outside. We can put them in the truck and store them for you for a fee, or you can take them. But for now, they're going outside."

"Why you do this? This is America. We are good people," he huffed. "There are children here. My grandchildren. You're taking their home away."

The officer ignored his questions. "Sir, please step outside," he said.

"Young man, I am almost eighty years old. I never see nothing like this," Abuelo complained half in Spanish, half in English. The officer shook his head. Vicky knew he didn't understand.

"Grab that small shoebox, *niña*," Abuelo said in Spanish, nodding toward one of the boxes she had seen the day he moved in. "It has your grandmother's pictures."

Vicky grabbed for the box and gently led him toward the door. She nearly stumbled at what she saw.

Their belongings were strewn in awkward piles in their front yard. The kitchen table, the place where all their family discussions and memories happened over the years, now sat in the middle of their brown lawn. Next to it sat an end table, a stool, and their kitchen chairs, arranged in a straight row. Lights, pillows, blankets were stacked atop each chair. Even their flat screen TV, which Dad bought a year before he lost his job, sat on the cement walkway like a piece of junk.

Cars passed by on the street. People eyed the police cruiser and the growing pile of items on the lawn. Vicky was sure everyone knew what was happening. She had heard of folks being evicted before. She knew if they weren't careful, people would steal their stuff.

Minute by minute, the pile grew. Even Mom and Dad's mattress now lay on its side in the driveway, like a dead animal.

Vicky sank onto the sofa, covering her face with her hands. She wanted to cry, but there were no tears left. Everything inside felt hollow and numb, as if all of her feelings had been sucked out by a giant vacuum.

At the sound of the engine, Vicky lifted her head. Her mother's car rounded the corner and skidded to a stop. Seeing her, Vicky felt a wave of relief. Maybe Mom could stop what was happening. Maybe she could tell them it was all a big misunderstanding.

But as Mom got out of the car slowly, Vicky could see the resignation in her eyes. She looked as if she was watching her whole life burn down and was powerless to stop it.

"I tried," she said, rushing right to Vicky. "I talked to everyone I could, but it was too late. Just like your father wrote." Her voice sounded raw and exhausted, and her face was worn with the same blank defeat Vicky felt inside. "All these months I thought we were paying the mortgage," she muttered. "I was paying only half of it. It would have taken twenty thousand dollars to stop this. *Twenty thousand dollars!* No one I know has that kind of money. I just wish your father would have told me. I wish we'd had some warning—"

"Look," Vicky interrupted.

A small form loped up the street toward the house. Vicky recognized it instantly.

Danny.

He was moving quickly until he saw the furniture in the yard. Then he stopped and gasped in disbelief.

"What's happening?" he shouted running toward them. "What are they doing?"

Mom grabbed him by the strap of his backpack to keep him from running into the house.

"Danny, Danny, listen to me—"

"They're taking all our stuff!" He struggled hard, yanking himself free. "We can't just stand here and let them—"

"For now, we have to," Mom said, trying to sound calm, even though she knew exactly how he felt. "Listen to me," she insisted, explaining everything that happened at the bank.

"I hate him," Danny hissed when she finished. "I *hate* him!" His eyes strayed away from her face, and Vicky turned to see the movers tossing a box of Danny's comic books onto the lawn.

"Hey!" Danny shrieked lunging toward them again. "Hey, that's mine! That's my stuff!" He raced across the lawn, gathering the box.

"I talk to him," Abuelo rose unsteadily, leaning heavily on his walker. "Remember what I tell you."

"Abuelo—"

Her grandfather waved her away, and moved slowly across the lawn toward her brother.

Mom leaned forward into Vicky, putting her arm on her shoulder, the

143

ruins of their home scattered all around them. Vicky grabbed her cross and prayed.

Please, Dad, she thought. *Just come home and make everything right. Please.*

The movers came out of the house empty-handed. The officer signed some paperwork, and they climbed into their truck and drove off. Moments later, a locksmith arrived. Vicky watched in silence as he locked her family out of their house forever.

"I'm sorry, folks," the officer said finally. "You have twenty-four hours to get this stuff off the property or you'll be fined. Of course if you leave it out on the curb, people might take it for you," he said, shrugging his shoulders. "Good luck," he added, sounding sincere as he rushed to his car. Within seconds, he was gone.

"What do we do now?" Danny asked.

No one answered. Mom shook her head wearily.

"What about our stuff?"

Vicky's skull pounded and throbbed.

"Where are we gonna go?"

"I don't know, Danny—just give me a chance to think!" Mom collapsed on a chair, and Vicky heard a car slowing to look at their yard strewn with belongings.

"Mom, there are apartments at Hill-side Manor," Vicky said, remembering the vacancy sign she had seen the other day. Danny looked up at her. That's where his best friend Mario lived. Martin too.

"We don't have enough money for a deposit," Mom replied. "Your Dad should've told me. Why didn't he tell me . . ." Her voice trailed off.

"Yes, we do," Abuelo said. "We have money."

"What are you talking about, Papi?"

Abuelo moved slowly and deliberately toward Vicky's mother. When he was close enough to touch her, he reached under his arm and pulled out the shoe-box he'd gathered earlier. "Here."

"What's this?"

"*Dinero*. Three thousand dollars. I offer it to Michael when I first came. He told me to keep it for you and the kids. I think he knew what was going to happen." Abuelo explained.

"But this was for your medicine, Papi—"

"No! Your mother and I save it for an emergency. Now, you take. Get my grandchildren a home. Please, don't refuse." He repeated the words in

Spanish. "For Vicky and Danny. Take it. Let me do this."

Mom looked into the box at the wad of bills inside. A war of emotions flashed across her face. Vicky knew her mother would normally refuse Abuelo's money. But now everything was different. Mom sighed and nodded her head. She looked pained.

"Thank you, Papi," she said in Spanish. "I'll pay you back, somehow. Danny, come with me. We might need Mario's mother as a reference," she said, putting her arm around his shoulder. Danny said nothing. He wandered to the car in a daze, as if the time bomb he had spray painted had blown up inside him.

As the car pulled away, Vicky sat next to her grandfather and looked at the shambles of her life. A stack of her clothing lay in a heap on the ground. In another little pile were some of the boxes she and Danny had unpacked just days ago. Vicky grabbed a few of them and began piling things into them: clothes and shoes, dishes and cleaning supplies, towels and sheets. She kept moving, anything to push out the gaping emptiness in her chest.

"Someone's coming," Abuelo said.

Vicky looked up, recognizing a familiar face walking down her block like a mirage.

Martin.

His mouth hung open in complete surprise. Seeing him, Vicky felt a wave of emotion flood through her. It was all just too much.

"Who's that?" Abuelo said.

"A friend," Vicky replied. Before she could say another word, Martin was at her side. He seemed to read her face. She felt his arms, strong and warm, wrap around her. She lowered her eyes into his chest and listened to his heart pounding. No matter what, she knew that he had come for her. Despite everything that happened, there he was. She drank in his embrace and felt her tears fall.

"I'm so sorry, Vicky," he said. "Teresa told me about your dad. That girl really has your back. I'm sorry I got everything so wrong. I didn't know you were dealin' with all this."

She couldn't speak. The wound in her chest was raw and open, too big for words. A wound so vast, nothing would ever wipe it away completely. But in that moment, Martin was with her. Finally, she wasn't alone.

"Listen," he insisted. "You stood with me when I needed you most. No one's ever done that for me. I'll stand with you, too. You hear me?" he said, touching her face. "Even if you wanted to get back with Steve, you're still going to have me as a friend. You understand?"

Vicky nodded and put her hands along the muscles of his back, pushing her face into the space under his chin.

"I don't want Steve," she said, turning her face up to his. He kissed her then, and she closed her eyes. And for a second, nothing existed except the warmth of his touch.

Just then, Vicky heard a familiar cough. Her grandfather's. He was behind them. Vicky gently pulled away.

"Shouldn't you introduce us?" Abuelo said in Spanish. Martin looked up in embarrassment. Vicky knew he understood.

"Yes, Abuelo," she said, smiling for the first time in days. "This is my friend, Martin Luna."

Mom came back, followed by a small white pickup truck. Mario and Danny were inside. Felix was behind the wheel.

Danny still seemed dazed, but Vicky was glad he had his friends, people who knew and cared for him. He wasn't alone either.

"We got a place three doors down from Mario," Mom announced as she got out of the car. Vicky could see that she was trying her best to sound cheerful, though her eyes were red and her face blotchy. Vicky was sure she had been crying as she drove the car back alone. "It's small, three little bedrooms and one bathroom. But we can afford it," she said.

Martin studied Mario's face. "He's my neighbor. That means—"

"I'm your neighbor too," Vicky added.

Martin tried to hide a smile. "You know what this means, don't you?"

Vicky shrugged.

"Your whole family is going to have to come over to our place for dinner."

Vicky winced at the words. Maybe they would go to Martin's one day. But it wouldn't be their whole family. Not with Dad gone.

She still couldn't believe what he had done. That he'd walked out. That he'd lied to them. That he wasn't coming back.

Just thinking about it brought tears to her eyes. She glanced back at the ruins of her family's home, its doors locked, its memories scattered in boxes and bags on the front lawn.

"You okay?" Martin said, looking at her.

Vicky nodded, pushing the tears back. Work needed to be done. The truck needed to be loaded. They needed to move.

"Martin, come here," Abuelo said. Martin rushed to join him.

Vicky watched as her grandfather introduced him to Mom and Danny. They shook hands and then Martin met Mario and Felix, who were getting ready to load the truck. Vicky almost couldn't believe it. She touched her grandmother's necklace as she watched them.

Something new was happening, something she had never imagined. Though it was laced with sadness and pain, there was something else there, too.

Friends. Family. A future.

Vicky took a deep breath, turned away from the empty house, and joined everyone.

They had work to do.

seeped into the soft material underneath the plastic, like blood spreading from a wound. Slowly, it grew darker and darker.

"Hello?" the voice yelled again.

Liselle cringed and shoved the cap back on.

"Go *away!*" she shouted.

The voice was young, too young to be a teacher's. *It's probably one of those kids who stay late for cheerleading or some other stupid club*, Liselle thought bitterly. Her ears were ringing, and a wave of nausea rose up in her stomach. She tried to think.

When was my last period? It's January now. November, maybe? October? She wasn't sure exactly, but it had been more than a couple of months. Liselle had tried to ignore this fact, figuring it would return as it had every month since she was twelve years old. But weeks had passed and her period never came. Then she noticed her jeans were getting snug around the waist. This morning, she couldn't even fit into her favorite pair.

Please, no, she thought looking at her face in the mirror before she left. *Were her cheeks fuller too?* she wondered. *Don't let it be that.*

was crumpled on the floor next to her. She laid her head on it, staring at the blue-and-white checkered tile. She wished she could just go to sleep and forget everything.

Since it was so late in the day, Liselle figured no one would come up to the remote third-floor bathroom. She had even pushed the heavy metal trash can in front of the door just in case, and then she locked herself in the last stall.

Clenched in her right hand was the long white plastic strip. Next to her was the white box. "Clear and Easy Pregnancy Test. Results in Five Minutes!" said the words in bold pink letters.

Has it been five minutes? she wondered.

She felt as if she had been sitting there for much longer. But each time she began to unclench her fist and look at the test, her heart would hammer in her chest like a furious drum.

"Just get it over with," she mumbled when she couldn't take it anymore.

Liselle sat up and yanked the cap off. Then she examined the tiny window. For a moment, she had trouble focusing her eyes. But then, from out of the stark whiteness, a blue plus sign appeared. It

Bang! Bang! Bang!

Liselle Mason winced. She sat alone on the cold tile floor of the girl's bathroom at Bluford High School. It was almost 4:00 on Friday afternoon. Most of the students had gone home. She knew Monique Reese, her best friend, was waiting for her in the SuperFoods parking lot just down the street. If she stayed much longer, Monique would wonder where she was.

"Hello?" a female voice yelled from the hallway. Liselle didn't recognize it. "Is anyone in there?"

Go away, Liselle whispered to herself.

Her hands shook and beads of sweat gathered on her forehead. Her backpack

Find out what happens next at

BLUFORD HIGH

The Test

Liselle Mason is in trouble. For weeks, she ignored the changes in her body and tried to forget her brief relationship with Oscar Price, her moody classmate at Bluford High. But when Liselle's clothes stop fitting, and her brother notices her growing belly, she panics. A pregnancy test confirms her biggest fears. Unwilling to admit the truth, Liselle suddenly faces a world with no easy answers. Where will she turn? Who will she tell? What will she do?

Turn the page for a special sneak preview. . . .

On her way to school, she had stopped in SuperFoods and walked down aisle seven, pulling the hood from her jacket over her head and turning up the music in her headphones. Then she had grabbed the same pregnancy test her cousin Shayna had taken last year. She remembered it because of the pink exclamation mark after the words "Results in Five Minutes!"

She had wanted to slip the box into her backpack and walk out without facing the cashier. But the store manager lingered at the end of the aisle fiddling with bottles of cough medicine. Liselle was sure he was watching her, so she paid for the test with a crumpled twenty-dollar bill she had taken from the tip jar in Mom's bedroom. Then she buried the small white box in her backpack and rushed out.

All day she had waited, pretending everything was fine, ignoring the dizziness she felt from time to time, especially when she stood up from her desk after class. When the final bell rang, she lingered anxiously at her locker until the hallways emptied out. Then she snuck into the third-floor bathroom, careful to make sure no one was following her.

She had told Monique that Mr. Mitchell, her English teacher, was making her stay after school to complete a missing homework assignment. She knew Monique would believe her. She was often kept late by one teacher or another.

But now what? she wondered, her hands cold and trembling. She hadn't told anyone of her suspicions, not Monique, not Oscar, and especially not Mom. The thought of Mom finding out made her cringe.

It has to be wrong, Liselle told herself. She popped off the cap of the test and studied it again. The plus sign was dark blue now, the color of a bruise.

No, she thought, her hands trembling. *It can't be right. I can't be pregnant.* She reread the directions on the back of the box: "A blue plus sign indicates pregnancy. 99% accurate results!"

The words taunted her. "*This test is never wrong!*" they seemed to say, "*You're pregnant, girl. So whatcha gonna do now?!*"